EDMUND GLASBY

◆

THE DOPPELGÄNGER DEATHS

Complete and Unabridged

LINFORD
Leicester

First published in Great Britain

First Linford Edition
published 2016

A catalogue record for this book is available
from the British Library.

ISBN 978–1–4448–3094–1

Published by

1

One Down, Five to Go

It was a few minutes after seven o'clock in the morning, and unshaven, unmarried, fifty-one-year-old Detective Inspector Gregory Vaughn was not in the best of moods. He lit a cigarette and threw away the match. Through a break in the hedge, he watched the other policemen, several hundred yards away, gather around the crashed dark-blue open-roofed convertible that had become entangled in a long trail of barbed wire.

He turned to the man beside him. 'So why the hell did you have to get hold of me? This is just a routine RTA, for Christ's sake.'

'Maybe, maybe not.' Thoughtfully, Richard Greene, the bespectacled crash investigator from the Greater Manchester Policing Unit, chewed at his bottom lip and looked around him. Expertly taking in his rural surroundings, he was able to mentally recreate the tragedy from the visible evidence: the tyre skid marks, the shattered glass, the nature of the damage caused, and the eventual position of the smashed-up vehicle.

Vaughn took a draw on his cigarette. 'What are you saying? You think it was something other than an accident?'

'That's for you to decide, not me,' Greene replied. 'Come on, there's something I want you to take a look at. Something that just doesn't make any sense. At least not to me.' Hands in his pockets, he set off.

Cursing at the prospect of getting his highly polished shoes muddied, Vaughn threw aside his cigarette and followed. There were deep tyre marks where the earth had been ploughed up. Entering the ragged, gaping hole in the hedge through which the vehicle had crashed after careering off the road, he saw the uprooted fence stakes from which the barbed wire had been ripped.

Greene waited for the detective to clamber over the obstacle. 'It would appear that the driver — Mr Keith Kemp, if his driver's license is anything to go by — either lost control of his vehicle or purposefully swerved to try and avoid something in the road. He clearly struck these bushes at some speed — perhaps sixty or seventy miles an hour, became enmeshed in the barbed-wire fencing, flipped once, maybe twice, and ended up where he did.'

'I don't suppose there were any witnesses to the crash, were there?' Vaughn asked hopefully.

'Doesn't seem to be. Least, no one's come forward. Bear in mind this isn't a very busy road and the crash occurred early in the morning. I believe it was reported by another motorist who came by a little later, a Mrs Hammett.' Greene removed his spectacles and gave them a wipe before putting them back on. 'I should warn you, it isn't pretty.'

'There's a surprise,' commented Vaughn dryly. Over the course of his career he had seen many road traffic accidents and many dead bodies, some more gruesome than others. Still, now

3

that he was nearing the wreckage, he was thankful that he had skipped breakfast that morning.

The driver's door hung wide and Kemp's battered and bloodied corpse, effectively garrotted and almost beheaded by barbed wire, lay slumped in its seat. The windscreen was cracked, and the sides of the car looked as though they had been viciously clawed by some fearsome creature. Both front wheels were buckled beyond recognition. The bonnet was crumpled, concertinaed out of shape.

Vaughn took in a deep breath. Scratching the stubble on his chin, he nodded. Greene had been right: it was not pretty. 'Jesus. What a way to go.'

'It gets better. Take a look.'

Intrigued, Vaughn stepped forward. Next to the unfortunate Kemp, and perfectly reposed in the heavily damaged passenger seat, sat a male porcelain doll of perhaps eighteen inches in size. A brown envelope was in its hands.

'What the hell?' It gave Vaughn the creeps and he felt queasy. Seeing a mangled human being was something he had mentally prepared himself for, but this was something else entirely — unsettling by its very incongruity. But there was more. For the doll, more an antique item than a child's plaything, was blood-spattered; and around its neck and upper body was fastened a loop of barbed wire.

'Weird, huh?' commented Greene. 'Didn't half give me the shivers when I first saw it.'

*   *   *

In his thirty years in the force, Vaughn had never known anything like it. He sat in his office, his eyes drawn once more to the piece of folded paper that had been found within the brown envelope, reading the simple message that had been inscribed in crude handwriting in black ink. It read: 'One down. Five to go.'

What had, on first impression at least, been nothing more than a fatal road traffic accident had now assumed the mantle of something far more sinister. Greene had been confident that, due to the damage and the fact that the car had flipped at least once before reaching its resting place, the doll and the envelope must have had been placed within the car post-accident. And, whilst that in itself did not immediately imply a murderous intention behind Kemp's death, it strongly suggested a hand in it. Yes, it could have been the action of a truly sick individual who had happened upon the crash before anyone else and had, for their own warped reasons, decided to place the doll inside the car — but surely the odds on that as an explanation were slim. And it lost all credibility when one considered the message. Everything pointed to murder.

At Vaughn's command, a search had been implemented to check if anything related had happened elsewhere. If this *was* murder, then it had been executed in an exceptionally brilliant way, which implied that whoever was responsible was very clever. Had it not been for the doll and the message, there was little reason to suspect it was anything other than a tragic accident.

There was a knock on the door just before it was opened. Ray Lockwood, the assistant forensic scientist, and Detective Sergeant Paul Tyler entered the office.

'Find anything?' Vaughn asked.

'Yes, indeed,' Lockwood replied. 'Seems that someone took a shot at Kemp. We were extremely lucky to find the bullet-mark, given the state of the wreckage. Unfortunately, though, there's no trace of the bullet itself, so we can't give you much more to go on. Still, given the location of the mark, just below the headlight on the driver's side, it would appear that the shot came from in front of the car.'

Vaughn reached for a pen and scribbled down some notes on a pad of paper. 'So it's quite likely that someone stepped out in front of the vehicle, took a shot at it whilst it was coming towards them — '

'Perhaps more than one,' Lockwood interrupted. 'As I said, it could be that there are other bullet-marks that we won't find. In addition, some may have missed entirely. All we can really say so far is that it was fired from a handgun of some kind.'

'But nothing hit Kemp, correct?'

'Hughes is finishing off his autopsy report, but there's nothing to suggest Kemp was shot,' Lockwood replied.

'It would appear, then, that sometime just after half-past five this morning Kemp left his house and set off to his place of work. On this occasion, though, someone chose to try and murder him by shooting him in his car, forcing him to swerve and crash.' From memory, Vaughn sketched a reasonably detailed plan of the crime scene. He ringed a part of the road he had drawn. 'It might be a good idea to do a search of this area here. Bullet casings. Footprints. Discarded cigarette ends. If we assume that whoever fired at the car is the same individual responsible for the doll, then they must've gone down to the crash site. Could be that there's something between the road and where the car ended up that we've missed. They must've left a trail of some sort. That field was as muddy as hell.'

'I'll get on to it straight away.' Dutifully, Tyler turned and left the office.

'That doll,' started Lockwood, 'is most unusual.'

'In what way?'

'Well, admittedly I'm not an expert on such things, but it's pretty clear that it's not your run-of-the-mill toy from Woolworths. In my opinion, I'd say it has to be at least a hundred years old. It's the kind of thing you sometimes hear about being sold at auction for thousands of pounds. Beats me why someone would leave it in the manner they did.'

'I'd have thought that was obvious. It's a 'calling card' of sorts. Why else would it be wrapped in barbed wire, imitating Kemp? Whatever sick bastard did this left it there as a sign of their handiwork. And what's more, it would appear that Kemp was only the first of six.'

*　*　*

Kemp's work colleagues had all been informed and interviewed, as had his sole remaining relative — a distant cousin who, at seventy-three — ten years the victim's senior, had little of any real relevance to impart. The deceased had worked as a financial clerk in Manchester and, whilst liked, had apparently lived a rather reclusive lifestyle. He had no known enemies, and a thorough search of his unassuming house had proved fruitless, yielding no clues whatsoever as to why someone would have wanted him dead.

As things currently stood, Vaughn was unable to establish any kind of motive, and that both puzzled and troubled him. What was even more concerning was the possibility that more murders, committed by the same perpetrator, could follow. He had spent much of the afternoon going through the paperwork. From Hughes's finalised autopsy report, it appeared that the cause of death was, not surprisingly, the severe lacerations inflicted by the barbed-wire 'noose' that had severed the jugular, resulting in massive blood loss. Kemp had also sustained a fractured pelvis, several broken ribs and a broken left radius. There was no indication of the victim having been shot.

Vaughn looked up as his office door was pushed open and Tyler entered. 'Sir, we've found some torn material snagged in the bushes near where the car came off the road. We've also found a trail of footprints leading from the road to the car, which may or may not belong to the killer. It's hard to be sure, as unfortunately the area was heavily trodden by some of the uniformed guys prior to it becoming a crime scene. Hughes is looking into some of the casts we've managed to collect. There's also been something of a breakthrough in finding a doll specialist. Lockwood's managed to track down an old university friend of his who fits the bill.'

'Excellent.' Vaughn rose from his chair. 'What about the handwriting? I know there's not much to go on, but has anyone come up with anything?'

Tyler shook his head. 'Nothing yet.'

'Okay.' Vaughn checked his watch, seeing that it was coming up to four o'clock. He was hoping to get away early, as it had been a long day. 'Obviously, we keep this under wraps for the time being.

If any reporters come knocking, this was just a bad RTA. Nothing more, nothing less.'

'Very good, sir.'

'Additionally, it might be a good idea to ensure that none of the bobbies who were on the scene this morning start spreading anything about. I know what rumours can fly in that canteen.'

'A bit late for that, I'm afraid, sir. PCs Theobald and Harris have already come up with the theory that the murder has something to do with witchcraft.'

'What?' The incredulity in Vaughn's face was clear to see. 'Witchcraft? Where the hell did they get that idea?'

'Can't rightly say, sir. Voodoo dolls, maybe?'

'Jesus Christ! This is the 1970s, for God's sake!'

'I'm just telling you what's being bandied around. After all, it was Theobald who was first on the scene. Guess seeing that doll in the passenger seat with barbed wire wrapped round its neck gave him quite a start.'

Briefly, Vaughn thought back to his first

sighting of Kemp's ghastly-looking inanimate passenger, and would be the first to admit it had had an unsettling effect on him too. He thought for a moment and, to his surprise, found himself entertaining the idea that maybe, just maybe, there was an occult link. He had read about such things: dolls crafted and fashioned into the likeness of living beings, then ritually destroyed — burnt or stuck with pins — in the belief that by so doing, a similar fate would befall the intended victim. But surely . . . No! He shook his head, dismissing the outlandish notion. Besides, the doll had been placed in the car after Kemp had died. Or had it?

'Sir?' Tyler asked uncertainly.

'Just thinking.' Vaughn was about to say something else when Lockwood turned up with a middle-aged woman with greying hair and thick glasses.

'Detective Inspector Vaughn,' said the assistant forensic scientist, 'may I introduce my friend Roza Weizak?'

Vaughn smiled. 'Good afternoon.'

'Good afternoon. Am I right in understanding that you have a doll you'd like me to take a look at?' It was clear that Roza was Polish, but her English was very good.

'That's right. Tyler, go and get it, would you?' Whilst the dispatched Tyler went to get the specimen in question, Vaughn fixed Roza a coffee. 'So you're an expert in dolls, are you?'

'I'd say an enthusiast rather than an expert.'

'Can't say I'm all that keen on them myself. I remember my sister had one when I was young and the damn thing creeped me out. You know what kids are like. She'd hide it under my bed or leave it under my heaped clothes. I ended up throwing the bloody thing in the canal.' Vaughn shuddered at some bad memory. 'Don't think she ever forgave me.'

'So you're a pediophobe?' Roza asked.

'Sorry?' Vaughn was taken aback.

'Someone with an irrational fear of dolls.'

'Oh. Yes, I suppose I was. When I was young of course.'

'But you said you're still not keen on them.'

14

Vaughn felt a touch uneasy. It was normally he who made others squirm by interrogating them. 'Well, there's just something about them. The eyes, I guess . . . and the unnerving smile.'

'Pediophobia's an ancient fear. According to Freud, such a fear stems from childhood and the belief that the doll, which is so often used as a toy — something to instil pleasure — can become real; that it can assume a life of its own. Did you know that an experiment was conducted in Russia at the time of Tsar Nicholas II, and — '

'Here we are, sir,' announced Tyler, entering the office. He walked forward and put the large cardboard box down on the desk. On the lid, written in thick black marker pen, was written 'Hamble'.

'Who did that?' demanded Vaughn, pointing to the box.

'Someone's idea of a joke, I'd say, sir,' Tyler replied. 'You know who Hamble is, sir?' He was trying hard to keep a straight face.

'Of course I do. It's the bloody doll out of *Play School*.' Tutting his disapproval,

Vaughn removed the lid and slid the now-opened box across to Roza.

The Polish woman's eyes lit up in astonishment. 'Good Lord!' Tentatively, she reached for it. 'May I . . . ?' Vaughn nodded. Almost reverently, Roza reached into the box and removed the doll. Carefully, she cradled it in her arms as though it were a living child. She winced upon seeing the blood and the coiled barbed-wire neck-tie.

'Well?' Vaughn asked.

'You've got something very special here. Austrian, German, possibly Bavarian. Mid-nineteenth century. At first I thought it was a Mersetz, but there's no characteristic dimple on the left wrist, so obviously that's not the case.' Roza ran her fingertips through the black hair and, raising the doll to her nostrils, took a sniff. 'Human. I thought as much.'

'The hair's human?' asked Vaughn in disbelief.

'Yes. That shouldn't come as much of a surprise, as it was quite common practice in doll manufacture.' Gently she spun the doll round, examining it from all angles.

'Not that there's anything else common about this. It's of a very high quality — the dress, the design, the facial features. Look at the detail on this little fox-headed tie pin. I've seen pictures of dolls a bit like this, and they were part of a distinct set.' Noting the confusion on the detective's face, she elaborated: 'Dolls such as this were generally found in what I'd call 'family units'. There would be a grandfather, a father, daughter, son and so forth. Often they would double up as marionettes, and little plays could be enacted.'

'So you think there's more of these out there?' asked Vaughn with interest.

'Quite likely.'

He nodded his head. Unbeknownst to her, the doll specialist had now confirmed his fears.

* * *

It had gone six in the evening by the time Vaughn got home. He fixed himself a simple meal and ate it in the kitchen before retiring to his study. His mind was

17

alive with the events of the day and all that he had seen. After Lockwood's Polish friend had left, he had called at the police morgue to see if Hughes had anything for him, but had largely drawn a blank. The pathologist had said it was nigh-on impossible to discern much from the flimsy pieces of evidence they had in their possession.

The cast impressions were of a poor and ambiguous quality. The handwriting appeared to belong to a male — so that narrowed it down to only fifty percent of the population — and the scrap of black material found caught in the bushes was currently undergoing 'further tests', but probably once belonged to a black coat.

Vaughn poured himself a whisky and sat down at his desk. There were so many aspects of this case which baffled him. Even though the car bore a bullet-mark, he was unsure as to whether or not it was murder; the bullet-mark could have been there for some time before the accident. Admittedly, all the facts, certainly as they stood, pointed to it being so; but without anything concrete to go on, he knew that was only speculation.

He gulped nervously as an image of the doll flashed through his mind. Like it or loathe it, as Lockwood's Polish friend had pointed out, something like that could fetch a tidy price even in its stained and slightly damaged condition. Indeed, she herself had made a not insubstantial offer for it.

There had been quite a bit of money in Kemp's wallet, and he had been wearing a nice watch. Clearly this 'homicide' had nothing to do with money, as so many did. Indeed, there was nothing as yet to provide any hint as to a motive.

Finishing his whisky, Vaughn lit a cigarette. He only smoked a few a day but found it helped him to think. He was wracking his brain for ideas, but nothing seemed to make sense. There were two questions that needed answering; he scribbled them down on a piece of paper.

'One — why did someone fire at Kemp's oncoming car?

'Two — why did he or she place a doll, made to appear dead in the same manner as the victim, within the car?'

And then there was the note. 'One down. Five to go.'

Unable to think of a motive, for the briefest of moments Vaughn found himself reflecting on the possibility of Kemp's death having been an elaborately planned suicide. However, that did not seem to make any sense when one considered the perfect placement of the doll. Surely if the victim had driven at speed through the bushes and the barbed-wire fence, it would have been lying in the footwell, having smashed against the windscreen. Besides, according to Greene, the car had flipped over at least once.

The evidence suggested that there was something profoundly disturbing at work. The more Vaughn went over the details, the more he became convinced that he was dealing with a truly disturbed individual — a psychopath, perhaps. The doll, the message and the bullet-mark all supported the theory that this was a premeditated murder, something that had been planned in advance and executed coldly and callously.

Vaughn had worked on a good many murders, but most of them had been spur-of-the-moment affairs, and some killers he had even felt some sympathy for. This death had an entirely different feel, however, and he had to admit, if only to himself, that it was one that sent a shiver down his spine.

The doorbell rang, its insistent chime an interruption that made Vaughn frown. It was nearly nine o'clock, and none of his neighbours were likely to disturb him at this time. He rose and answered the door.

'Sorry to trouble you at home, sir.' Constable Wilkes was standing outside, still in uniform. 'Detective Sergeant Tyler sent me round with this.' He held out a slim package.

'That's all right, Wilkes. Are you going off duty now?' Vaughn asked, taking the package.

'Yes, sir. I live fairly nearby.'

'Okay. Thanks.'

Vaughn took the package inside and opened it. There was a scribbled note that read: 'We finally found a recent photograph of the victim.' Picking up the picture, he saw a neatly — one could say pedantically — dressed man with slicked-down dark hair and a rather thin neck. His mouth was slightly pursed, and there was a hint of impatience in his eyes. The image would have been completely unremarkable had it not been for the polaroid that Tyler had included in the envelope. Vaughn had already felt a shock of recognition when he saw the picture of Kemp, but the two images laid side by side made it clear. From the dark hair to the facial expression, and even to the wrinkles painted on the porcelain face, the doll was a dead ringer for the deceased.

2

The Austrian Connection

The news coverage of the death of Keith Kemp had at first been lacklustre. Yet another victim of a road traffic accident, the local press had assumed, in the absence of further information. Vaughn had been granted a brief reprieve before the unsettling details began to leak out. By the morning of the third day, however, several reporters had turned up at the station, hoping to verify the rumours they had picked up about a maniac who had left a doll as a calling card.

'How do they get wind of these things?' Tyler asked incredulously. He and Vaughn were discussing the progress they had made so far, or rather the lack of it.

'People gossip,' Vaughn replied tersely. 'If I find out it was one of our lot, they'll be for it. But it could be quite a few others; the woman who reported the crash, for a start.'

'Susan Hammett? Could be.' Tyler turned the possibility over in his head. 'She went to check if anyone was hurt, didn't she? I suppose if I'd seen that bloody doll sitting next to the corpse, I'd find it hard to keep my mouth shut too.'

'At least we had them off our backs for a day or two.' Vaughn accepted the inevitability of press intrusion as being part of the job, even a useful part sometimes, but he never felt comfortable around reporters. Quite apart from feeling that they were trying to trip him up, he resented the fact that they got excited about gruesome cases. An old girlfriend had once accused him of making his living from tragedy, just before she left him, but at least he was trying to find justice for the victims and prevent further deaths. The worst of the gutter press wanted more deaths to increase their readership.

'Forget them for the moment,' he advised Tyler. 'We have to concentrate on the job at hand. We've a victim who seems to have led a blameless life. He only left a small amount of money to his cousin as his house was rented, and he didn't seem to have annoyed anyone at work enough for them to resort to murder.'

'Everyone has secrets, though,' Tyler mused. 'Maybe someone from his past?'

'Quite possibly. I've got a brief history of his life: schools, jobs, and some information about his parents. In the absence of any other leads, we'll need to find out everything we can. There must be some reason he was killed and some reason for the doll.' Vaughn leant back in his chair and looked up at the ceiling, his favourite position for thinking. 'The fact that it looks quite like the victim can't be a coincidence, so the killer must have been planning this for a long time — long enough to find an antique in the image of Kemp.'

'Roza Weizak said that she would send us a list of dealers who might have handled such a sale. I can chase her up for it.'

'She has a shop near here, doesn't she?' Vaughn asked.

'Yes. Hang on a minute.' Tyler flipped back through his notebook. 'Here it is. Bedwin Street.'

'Okay. Keep Fuller working on Kemp's background; try to find an old school friend we can talk with. Then meet me in the car park and we'll see if Miss Weizak has anything for us.'

'What about the press?'

'I'll talk to the chief superintendent later and we'll try and cobble together some kind of statement; keep them happy for a while.' Vaughn rose from his chair. 'The only benefit I can see of having a chief superintendent like Bernard Wishbourne is that he's good at making a little information go a long way. At least the contents of the envelope haven't been leaked yet. 'One down. Five to go' — Hell, the papers would have a field day with that.'

He glanced at the photographs of Kemp and the doll that he had pinned on the wall, hoping they were not just the beginning.

★   ★   ★

The door of the quaintly named *Roza's Rarities* opened with a jingle of bells, allowing Vaughn and Tyler access to the main room of the shop. To Vaughn's surprise, it was not the usual stuffed-to-the-gunnels kind of antique shop that his mother had sometimes taken her children round. This was more sparingly laid out and had an underlying theme that unified the room. It was an almost perfect example of regency furniture and art, and he found it far more tasteful than the eclectic mix of eras and styles that he had expected.

The bells had prompted Roza to appear from a side room and she smiled in welcome. 'Hello, Inspector Vaughn. Sergeant Tyler. Or is it Chief Inspector? I'm a little confused by English police terms.'

'Inspector's fine, Miss Weizak,' Vaughn assured her. People rarely got it right and he only corrected them if they were being difficult. 'I was hoping you might have that list of dealers for us.'

'Of course. I was going to call Ray — Mr Lockwood — later to say it was ready. It took me a little time to ask around. Do sit down while I get it for you.' She waved them towards the dining table set up with antique candelabras and cutlery.

'There's some nice stuff here. I might bring the missus round to pick up a few things,' Tyler said as he reached out to turn over the price tag on a silver bowl. His eyebrows went up as he saw the amount. 'Or then again, maybe not.'

'Not on your current salary, at any rate,' Vaughn agreed. 'Or mine, for that matter.'

Roza returned with a handwritten sheet of paper and handed it to Vaughn. 'Here they are. These five dealers all specialise in toys, and they would know about any auctions that have taken place in this country in the last ten years or so. This one — ' She pointed to the last name on the list. ' — has an international business and would be able to put you in touch with auction houses in Europe and America.' She beamed at the two men. 'I'm an amateur when it comes to dolls, but these men have real expertise.'

Vaughn looked down the list, checking that he could read all the details clearly. Satisfied, he rose and put the sheet in his pocket. 'Thank you, Miss Weizak. This is most helpful.'

'Do you really think there's a connection between the doll and that poor man in the car?' she asked, her smile fading. 'The story in the papers was . . . rather disturbing.'

'We're exploring every possibility,' Vaughn answered with the usual tired old line.

'Of course, you can't tell me,' Rosa said apologetically.

The detectives repeated their thanks and turned to leave, but Vaughn could detect an unasked question hanging in the woman's mind. He paused for a moment at the door and looked back. Sure enough, she took a step towards him.

'You may not know this, Inspector, but there are some people who get quite odd about dolls. They start to attribute human feelings to them, much as a child would.'

'Oh, yes?' Vaughn replied encouragingly.

'I myself am very fond of dolls and old toys, but I would never refuse to sell one of mine for the right offer. For some, however, they become part of the family. They became strongly attached to them. When Mr Lockwood told me how that doll you have had been placed at the scene of the accident, it gave me the shivers. Imitations of human beings, which is what dolls are, can invoke odd emotions in some.'

'Like voodoo dolls?' Tyler blurted out.

'Well, a little like that,' Roza reluctantly agreed.

'Do you know anyone who has an unhealthy attitude to dolls, Miss Weizak?' Vaughn asked.

'I've met a few over the years, but not to remember their names, I'm afraid. My main interest is in furniture. The list I gave you may be of assistance, though. I would suggest you start with Humphrey Grace. He's the most respected expert in Britain, and if your doll has been sold anytime within his memory he'd be able to tell you who bought it.'

Vaughn thanked her again and they left the shop.

'She's a bit spooked by this,' Tyler commented.

'Maybe she's wondering if any of her doll-loving acquaintances are secretly murderers,' Vaughn said, taking the sheet of paper from his pocket. 'This Humphrey Grace lives in Penzance. That's too far to justify visiting him at the moment. I'll call him when we get back, and we can get a set of photos sent down; see if he recognises it. The other experts too. We can split the phoning between us.'

They reached the car and Vaughn sat for a few moments, considering his next move. Tyler, who was used to the occasional silences, waited patiently.

'Okay,' Vaughn finally said. 'By the end of tomorrow I want us to have as full a biography of Kemp as possible, and to have established contact with each of these doll experts. I can't see forensics coming up with anything new at this stage, unless someone finds a bullet. I want to know everything about Keith Kemp. There has to be some reason he was killed like this.'

'It isn't necessary to prove motive to convict someone,' Tyler said lightly.

'I know that,' Vaughn grunted. 'Just the means and opportunity. But I need to have some suspects to investigate, and at the moment I can only narrow it down to anyone who possesses or has access to a gun. Do you know how many British citizens that covers?'

'Too many,' Tyler admitted.

'Right. So I'm hoping there's someone in Kemp's past or present with a reason to kill him, or it's unlikely we'll ever get anywhere.'

'Unless there's another murder,' Tyler said grimly.

Vaughn started the car and pulled out from the parking bay. 'The press may think that way, but we're not supposed to.' In the privacy of his mind, however, he could not help but agree.

★　★　★

The details they had gathered about Kemp's life indicated that he had been average in every way — a diligent but not brilliant schoolboy, a perfectly competent employee, a decent friend. Everyone who had been questioned was of the opinion that he was 'very normal'. Asked by Tyler why Kemp had never married, one of his work associates had said that the man seemed to prefer freedom to companionship, saying that he got on all right with women but did not want to be tied down.

'This is hopeless!' Tyler complained. 'There's no one who either loved or hated him enough to kill him.'

'There was at least one person,' Vaughn reminded him. 'We just have to keep digging.'

The antique dealers had all been contacted and agreed to look at the photographs when they received them. By mid-afternoon on the day the pictures would have reached them, four of the five had called the station. All confirmed the information Roza had given but had nothing new to add. Vaughn decided he could wait no longer for the last expert, Humphrey Grace, and called him. Grace answered almost immediately.

'Mr Grace, it's DCI Vaughn. We spoke yesterday. I wondered if you'd received the photographs yet.'

'Yes, I'm looking at them right now. It's a remarkable piece, you know.' The dealer sounded incredibly frail, but enthusiastic.

'Have you seen it before?' Vaughn pressed.

'Well ... I don't think so, but something about it is familiar. I just can't put my finger on it. I'm certain it's not one we've sold, at any rate. I've seen a female doll rather like this one, many years ago when I was working in Austria, but I don't think that's what's ringing a bell with me.'

'Is it valuable?' Vaughn asked.

'Definitely. Your photographs are rather good, and I can see the workmanship is excellent. It's reminiscent of Mersetz, but with slightly more flair I'd say. Even though it's slightly damaged and without provenance, I'm confident it would do well at auction. Not that it would appeal to everyone.'

'I can understand that,' Vaughn said,

rather more forcefully than he had intended.

'Absolutely. People want dolls to be life-like, but this kind of doll, and the kind that Mersetz produced, is almost too human to be attractive. They're more akin to portraits. Indeed, it's quite possible that they were actual portrayals of real people known to the makers. I'd love to sell one, but I'm not sure that I'd want to own one.' Grace paused. 'I just wish I could work out why this feels familiar.'

'Both you and Miss Weizak mentioned the name Mersetz. Who is that, exactly?'

'Joseph Mersetz was a doll-maker in the nineteenth century, based in Vienna but popular in England as well. He specialised in these sorts of very real faces that are almost unsettling. The dolls were of a beautiful quality, as were the clothes and accessories that came with them. Each of his creations has a characteristic dimple on one of the hands, as well as a maker's mark hidden underneath the clothes. I can see from the photographs that there is no dimple on your doll, so it's very unlikely to have been one of his.

It may quite possibly have been made by one of his apprentices, either as a test of his skill or for selling at a lower price. I couldn't say more without seeing it, I'm afraid.'

'Well, my interest in the doll is more to do with its owner,' Vaughn admitted. 'Someone must have bought it fairly recently.'

'I'm quite sure that it hasn't come up in any of the major sales of the last few years. I would have heard about it.' Grace paused a little awkwardly. 'When you called me yesterday, you just said that you needed some information about a doll. I rather assumed that it had turned up as stolen goods, but there's a rumour going round that it has something to do with a death, possibly a murder.'

Vaughn reflected that the local newspapers' scoop was spreading. It had not made the national news yet, to his knowledge, but doubtless experts like Grace had a lot of acquaintances around the country.

'I can't tell you any details, but yes, there is a connection,' he answered.

'What an unpleasant thought. If what I've heard is correct, and I won't ask you to confirm it, then I can see why you would like to trace the doll's history. Who else have you contacted?'

Vaughn reeled off the list Roza had given him, which met with Grace's approval.

'That's the main British ones taken care of. If you like, I can call a couple of dealers in Europe to ask around. I can give a very good description from these photographs.'

'Thank you. That would be a help.'

'Of course, it may be that this doll has been in private ownership for years, in which case it's unlikely that any of us would know of it,' Grace warned.

'Well, if you do find anyone who recognises it, let me know.'

Vaughn made sure that Grace had his phone number and then rang off. He looked down at the note on his desk with some distaste. Chief Superintendent Wishbourne wanted a progress update on the case. As the only progress they had made was negative, he did not relish the task, but it could not be put off.

Bernard Wishbourne, generally known as 'Windbag Wishbourne' behind his back, was not particularly popular with either the rank-and-file or the plain-clothes police. He had certainly served his time on the force, and was not short of experience, but he had set his sights on the administrative side of policing early on and had been out of touch with life at the coalface for twenty years. Nearing retirement, he had a tendency to lecture people about how it was done better in his day, and was grudging with praise — very few officers seemed to live up to his nostalgic vision of how they should be. On the other hand, he tended to side with the police against the outside world, particularly against the press.

Vaughn picked up his rather meagre file of information on the case and squared his shoulders for the inevitable lecture.

* * *

The chief superintendent's office was too warm, and his voice rumbled along on the usual well-worn tracks. Having brought Wishbourne up to date with the investigation — a fairly brief task, Vaughn was struggling to stay alert. His mind kept drifting back to the crime scene — the dreadful lacerations from the barbed wire on Kemp's neck and the unsettling neatness of the doll beside him. He found his hand going to his own neck in unwitting sympathy, and dragged his attention back to the present.

'In order to keep the wolves from the door, I'm going to have to give the press a report tomorrow, you know, Vaughn,' Wishbourne was saying. 'I'll need enough meat to keep them happy.'

Vaughn nodded in agreement. 'I'll ask Tyler to write up the salient points for you, sir. It may be best to hint that we're only releasing minimal details to safeguard an important line of enquiry.'

'And are we?' Wishbourne demanded.

'Well, I'm hoping that these antique specialists might come through with some useful information, and we've started to trawl through the list of firearm licensees. But I have to admit that apart from that, there's very little to go on.' Vaughn grimaced at the admission. They really were running out of leads.

Wishbourne leaned back in his chair and interlaced his fingers, almost in prayer. 'I'll be retiring in — ' He glanced at the small calendar on his desk. ' — seven months from now, and I don't want a high-profile unsolved murder to be the last big thing on my record. We can put extra people onto this case, so bring in experts, whatever you need, Gregory. Just get it sorted and you'll have my highest recommendation.'

And if I don't, you'll feed me to the wolves, Vaughn thought. It always irked him when the chief superintendent called him by his first name. There was nothing wrong with the 'last names only' policy at work, and it felt like an intrusion for his boss to use the name that he preferred to reserve for family and a very few friends.

Recognising that the interview was over, he left and headed for the morgue.

★ ★ ★

The underground set of rooms that comprised the morgue were as usual rather cold, and it helped to wake Vaughn up. His main reason for descending to the basement was to quiz Hughes, the pathologist. His report had been completed but informed Vaughn of nothing he did not already know. Kemp had died suddenly from the massive injuries to his neck. There had been no alcohol or drugs in his system, and he had been of average health for a man of his age. The body could not tell them any more at the moment.

Tom Hughes was a small man. His fair hair had faded almost imperceptibly into grey and then got thinner and thinner until it was now only clinging on above his ears. He had slim, precise hands that he kept scrupulously clean, and he wore thick spectacles to combat his poor eyesight. Vaughn had seen him bloodied to the elbow, painstakingly sifting through the remains of a victim of violent death with a look of quiet satisfaction on his face. Some found him creepy, a cold fish, and called him 'Dr Frost'; but Vaughn had long ago realised Hughes was as compassionate as the next man — he just had a strength of focus on his work that helped him to see each corpse as a puzzle waiting to be solved.

They had worked on a particularly nasty murder a decade earlier, and although Hughes had delivered his evidence with dispassionate clarity as an expert witness, he had uncharacteristically stayed to hear the final verdict. As the life sentence was handed out with provisos that ensured the unrepentant murderer would never be free again, Vaughn had seen the look of hatred and disgust that they had all felt displayed on Hughes's usually placid face. Many officers expressed their animosity towards criminals vocally, venting their anger through claims that they would crucify the bastards. Hughes merely settled his glasses on his nose and carefully picked his way through the bodies, gathering the evidence that would provide the nails.

'Hello, Tom,' Vaughn said, walking into the small office where the pathologist wrote his reports. As usual, there was a half-finished crossword on the desk. 'Any good clues today?'

Hughes looked up, peering over his glasses. 'A couple of interesting ones, if you mean the puzzle. But if you mean the case, I'm afraid we've drawn a bit of a blank.'

Vaughn sat down in the free chair and helped himself to a biscuit from the packet Hughes offered to him. 'I know. I've told Tyler off for hoping for another body to get us further along, but to be honest it's probably our best bet. I was wondering if you had any ideas, though — off the record.' Vaughn raised his eyebrows suggestively.

'Speculation is frowned upon in my occupation, as you well know. If you can't prove it, it's not permissible.' Hughes tapped his manicured fingers on the faded wood of the desk. He was known to bleach it regularly, and the room often smelled of disinfectant. 'If I were to speculate, however, just between old friends, I'd say that the killer of Mr Kemp is decidedly strange.'

'I've worked that out for myself.'

'What I mean is this is *authentically* strange — deranged, if you like. Do you remember the Ivy Culpepper Case?'

'The woman who killed her lodger back in the fifties?'

'That's the one. She'd tried to frame his girlfriend, of whom she was of course jealous, and knew that the poor woman had had some psychotic incidents in her past. So she arranged an elaborate scene of evisceration where each internal organ had been carefully removed and wrapped in silk before being returned to the corpse.'

'The girlfriend worked as a seamstress, didn't she? And Culpepper had got hold of some of her supplies,' Vaughn said as he recalled the bizarre crime.

'The idea, of course, was to suggest the murder could only have been committed by someone insane; and she fooled everyone for a while, even to the point where the girlfriend admitted herself to a mental institution, half-convinced that she *had* done it.'

'You helped out in that case, didn't you?' Vaughn asked.

'Called in for a second opinion by a colleague who felt that something was wrong,' Hughes confirmed. 'We went over all the forensic evidence with the investigating officer and we both had the feeling that it didn't ring true. Of course, we were lucky that a witness came forward who could prove that the girlfriend had been miles away at the time of death, and Culpepper's alibi turned out to be false. Once we knew what to look for, the clues were there, and they eventually convicted her of murder.'

'So how does that relate to this case?'

'Culpepper's mistake was trying too hard to make the murder look like the work of a madman, or mad*woman* to be precise. But the death of Keith Kemp feels like the real deal to me.' Hughes wiped a few biscuit crumbs from his fingers with a handkerchief. 'I'm leaving for the day, since there's nothing more I can do for now.' He folded up the crossword and they left the basement together.

Climbing the stairs, they heard a heightened level of activity in the station.

Long years of experience told them that something significant had happened. Hughes exchanged a look with Vaughn. 'I've a feeling your Friday night plans may be cancelled.'

Sure enough, Tyler came walking briskly along the corridor towards them. 'We've had a report come through just now, sir. A death at a factory along Cobb Street.'

Vaughn tensed. 'What kind of death?'

'The owner was found floating in a wastewater tank, and when our boys got there one of them spotted a sodden object in the tank with him. They haven't touched it yet, but they're sure it's another one of those dolls.'

Vaughn felt a rush of adrenaline that eliminated any trace of tiredness. 'Come on, then, let's get over there. Tom — '

'I'll meet you there. I need to get my kit and pick up Lockwood,' Hughes interrupted him, turning back towards the basement stairs. 'Looks like my bridge night's cancelled too.'

'Do you know anything about the victim?' Vaughn asked Tyler as they walked to the car.

'According to the constable who radioed it in, he's called Malcolm Forrester — and I'm quoting here: 'It's only a wonder no one topped the bastard before.''

3

Death of a Crook

'What a dump!' Tyler commented. They had pulled up outside a dismal-looking brick building that must have been a hundred years old. It had none of the charm of some of the Victorian factories that still survived in parts of the city. Instead, the dark walls just loomed above them.

'What is it they make here?' Vaughn enquired.

'No idea, sir. I've never been down this way before.' Tyler looked with distaste at the factory. 'It's all a bit 'dark satanic mills'. I mean, look at all that rubbish.' He pointed to the large heap of assorted bits of twisted metal and junk piled up against one side of the building. 'PC Warren and the others should be inside somewhere.'

They found what was probably the

main entrance — although there was no business name to verify it — and pushed open the heavy door. Inside was a hallway, with a clocking-in system for the workers.

Vaughn made a rough estimate of the number of cards. 'Looks like they have about thirty men. I suppose the place is in shut-down today.'

'Well, it is after five o'clock. They might've already finished for the day,' Tyler pointed out.

They walked through a set of double doors at the end of the hall and came out into a cavernous space. There were conveyor belts, hoppers, small work-benches and stacks of raw materials. It would normally have been a hive of activity, but now all the machines were silent. There were only a few men standing in the centre, with two uni-formed police on guard.

Vaughn approached the officers. 'Okay, give me the details, Warren.'

'Yes, sir. PC Mayther and I were patrolling on Golbrook Road when the station radioed us with reports of a death in the factory. We were the nearest, so we were here within five minutes. There was the body of a man in a big water tank. It's through there.' He nodded to the left, towards another door. 'He'd obviously been dead some time, so we got everyone back from the scene and called for you.' The constable was choosing his words carefully, intentionally not looking at the small gathering of workers.

'Okay, let's have a look then. Mayther, you stay here. Dr Hughes will be along shortly.'

Warren led his two superiors through the door and into a smaller room with a large circular tank in it. It was about seven feet in diameter and four feet high.

'The body's in here,' Warren added rather unnecessarily.

Floating face down in the scummy water, which stank of oil, was the body of Malcolm Forrester. There was a nasty-looking wound on the back of his head indicative of a heavy blow. The skin had been broken and a portion of skull was visible.

'How sure are you that this is Mr Forrester?'

'He was found by the foreman, Gerry Nielson, who said he was one hundred percent sure it was his boss.'

'Did he see the face?' Vaughn persisted.

'I believe so,' Warren replied, his eyes flicking to the tank.

'Okay. We'll still need a formal identification, but that will do for now. What about the doll? I can't see anything.'

'It was PC Mayther who spotted it. You have to lean over a bit.' Warren pointed to the inner side of the tank. 'Down there.'

Vaughn peered into the water. At first he could see nothing but the edges of the tank, but after a moment he heard a muffled exclamation from Tyler and saw it himself: a small white face staring up through the water.

* * *

The sodden corpse had been photographed and finally fished out of the tank. Hughes and Lockwood had arranged it

51

on a plastic sheet. The doll had also been removed and laid beside the man, in the process of which a now-familiar brown envelope containing a letter, partially disintegrating but still just about legible, had been found. The room was being checked for any traces left behind by the killer, and the remaining factory workers were eager to leave.

While he waited to get Hughes's preliminary findings, Vaughn had begun to interview the men, using the main office as an ad hoc interview room. The foreman, Nielson, had been first — a large, muscular man who had undoubtedly been shaken by the death of his employer. He had kept slightly apart from the other men, Vaughn had noticed, and when he was alone with the two detectives he got straight to the point.

'It'll be one of them that did it,' Nielson pronounced belligerently, jerking his thumb toward the room where the other workers were gathered. 'You've got my full support. Whatever you need. I know all the dirt.'

'What makes you say that, Mr Nielson?' Vaughn was always wary of accusations as, in his experience, they were seldom right. They did, however, tell him a lot about the accuser.

'It's that bloody commie, Burns! He's been agitating ever since he got here. Nothing's right for him — the hours are too long, the machinery's too old, not enough tea breaks.' Nielson was getting worked up. 'He's bloody lucky he's even got a job! There's plenty round here would be grateful for it, but he's been stirring things up.'

'Can we go back a bit and hear about how you found the body?' Vaughn asked calmly. 'Take me through it.'

'Okay.' Nielson let out an explosive breath of air and tried to compose himself. 'It was getting on for the end of the day, and I always do a round of the building — make sure the lads haven't left stuff out of place, that kind of thing. You see, we don't use that room for anything much. It's just the dirty water from the cleaning process. It builds up over about ten days, and then we let it all drain out to the sewer.'

'It must be nearly at the ten-day mark, judging by how full it is.'

'That's right. I would have flushed it on Monday. Everywhere else was fine, but when I went in there I saw him immediately. To tell the truth, I don't think I did anything for a couple of minutes. I couldn't really take it in. Then I started shouting to the others to shut everything down. It's a noisy factory, and suddenly all that sound was getting to me.' The foreman stopped and breathed hard. The shock was obviously still with him.

'At what point did you realise the victim was Mr Forrester?' Vaughn asked.

'Instantly. First thing I did was see if he was still alive; see if I could revive him. But I could see it was hopeless. Poor bugger had been dead for hours.'

'Did anyone else see the body?'

'Yeah, when I came to the office to call you lot they all piled in to gawp. I had them out of there sharpish as soon as I was off the phone, and they've been in the main room ever since.'

Vaughn frowned. This would make it a lot harder for any evidence they found to be firmly linked to the murderer; and if the killer was any of the employees, it would have been to their advantage to join in the general scrum to see the body. But what about the doll? As far as Vaughn knew, none of them had noticed the porcelain interloper, which was a blessing for him. The longer they could keep that under wraps, the better. Its presence at the crime scene made it less likely that one of them had killed Forrester, but it could of course be a red herring. Someone with a grudge against the boss could have tried to throw suspicion on the killer of Kemp.

'Okay, so tell me about Mr Forrester and why you think one of his employees might have done this,' Vaughn said.

Tyler had to write fast to take notes of all the bile that came spilling out of Nielson. According to the foreman, Forrester was the classic firm but fair boss, and people should have been grateful they had a job at all, rather than complaining about non-existent dangers.

The trouble had started a few months ago when one Cyril Burns had been taken on as a machine operator. At first he had kept his head down, but soon Nielson had noticed a change in the atmosphere. On several occasions he had walked into the tearoom and had the impression a conversation had been hastily dropped. Then the demands had started. Forrester had been bombarded with questions each time he had come to the factory. He mostly shrugged them off, but Burns was persistent. Nielson and Forrester had discussed what to do about the agitator and had been going to fire him. They had a job, a big order from British Rail that needed to be completed by the end of the month. As Burns was a highly skilled worker when he wanted to be, Forrester had decided to wait until the job was finished before giving him the boot.

'Did Burns know about this plan?' Vaughn interrupted the flood of invective.

'I don't know. Neither of us would have let it slip, but he must have got wind of it or he wouldn't have done this. You get that bastard in here and ask him yourself!'

'I'll be talking to everyone in due course, Mr Nielson, and my officers are not going to let anyone leave.' Vaughn regarded the foreman with a calculating eye. The man was big enough and strong enough to have killed Forrester himself. His righteous anger could be masking guilt. It was too early to know. 'What do you know of Mr Forrester's home life?' he asked, turning the conversation in a different direction.

'He lived with his wife and they have two grown-up sons.'

There was a knock on the door and Lockwood entered. 'We have the initial information for you, sir,' he said.

'Thank you,' Vaughn replied. He turned back to Nielson. 'I think that's all for the moment, but I'd like you to hang on for a bit if you don't mind. We need to take prints from all of you.' Nielson scowled, but nodded and left the small office they were using for interviews.

'Tell them to keep an eye on him,' Vaughn muttered to Tyler. 'He could kick something off with Burns.'

A minute later they were both looking

down at the pale body of Malcolm Forrester, a late middle-aged bald man with a ginger moustache and mutton-chop sideburns. The resemblance to the doll beside him was undeniable, for it too bore the same facial hair and features.

'Okay, Tom. What've you got for me?' Vaughn asked.

Hughes was standing by the corpse and carefully peeling off his gloves. 'Well, he may have drowned, but I won't know till I've opened up his lungs.' He pointed to the battered head. 'However, that concussive blow probably killed him outright, and then the killer decided to dump him in the tank. Certainly most people wouldn't have survived it. I'd guess he's been dead between eight and twelve hours. Do you know how often this room is used?'

'Nielson said that he checks the building at the end of each day, and there was no reason for anyone to enter the room earlier than that,' Tyler said, consulting his notes.

'Well that doesn't help us much. Of course, we only have Nielson's word for it

58

that he doesn't check the room in the mornings. If he's the killer, he'd want to fudge the timing.' Vaughn looked at the puffy features and staring eyes of the corpse. Then he moved his attention to the doll. He shivered, noticing the similarities. The resemblance was uncanny. 'Christ . . . that's unreal,' he mumbled. 'It's almost as though the doll was modelled on him.'

'I know what you mean — and have you noticed the crack on the back of its head?' said Hughes. Vaughn nodded. 'It's in almost exactly the same position as the blow that Mr Forrester sustained. I'll get back to the station now and open him up. If you can find me some information about when he last ate, that would be a help in establishing a time of death.'

'Time to visit the next of kin?' Tyler asked.

Vaughn considered his next move. He needed to speak to Mrs Forrester. There was no doubt about that, but it was often wiser to wait until the first shock of murder had passed, at least when the person you were interviewing was unlikely to be the killer. He knew that a couple of uniformed officers had been dispatched to break the news to the family, and judged that he could safely leave them until the morning. Burns, however, was a different matter.

His mind made up, he asked Tyler to bring the agitator to the office.

* * *

Cyril Burns was in his mid-thirties, with springy black hair and a slightly Mediterranean look to him. He seemed calm, but Vaughn thought he could detect tension underneath, though not more than was usual for a person suddenly thrust into a murder investigation.

'Mr Burns, can you tell me what you thought of your employer?' Vaughn began.

'I was expecting something more like 'where were you between the hours of ten and twelve last night,'' Burns replied with a raised eyebrow. His accent and style were more refined than Vaughn had expected, and several steps higher up the class ladder than Nielson.

'At the moment I would just like your impressions of Mr Forrester,' Vaughn said neutrally.

'All right. He was intelligent, hard-working and, most probably, kind to his dogs — he bred retrievers, you know.' Burns paused and his tone of voice hardened. 'As an employer, though, I thought he was overbearing, aggressive, exploitative and borderline criminal. I've been trying to organise the other workers here to demand better conditions, and I've repeatedly brought safety issues to his notice, but neither endeavour has been successful. They worry too much about losing their jobs, and he doesn't, or rather didn't, give a damn about anything but money. I could go on, but that's the general thrust of my problems with Mr Forrester.' He sat back in the chair, looking defiant.

Vaughn wondered where to begin. Burns had surprised him — not with his views on Forrester, but by his whole personality. From Nielson's description, he had been unconsciously imagining a working-class firebrand big on rhetoric and passion but short on self-control. In contrast, Burns was very collected, very precise and very slightly unsettling. Vaughn felt a small germ of excitement as he admitted to himself that he knew of several killers who had possessed the same qualities. Burns had clearly hated Forrester, and the whole doll business could have been nothing but a smoke-screen.

'I imagine that Nielson hasn't been singing my praises,' Burns said sarcastically.

'What makes you say that?' Vaughn asked.

'Call it a hunch. We don't really see eye to eye.'

'Would you care to expand on that?'

'Nielson thought the sun shone out of Forrester's backside,' Burns said bluntly. 'According to him, those poor sods who work here should have been tugging their forelocks whenever the great man walked by. Of course, given Nielson's background, he was lucky to get any job, let alone one that suited his temperament so well.'

'And what would that background be?'

'GBH. Nielson was an enforcer for the notorious Halliwells a good few years ago.' Burns sat back smugly, watching for a reaction.

'That would be Ron Halliwell's gang, I take it?' Vaughn said mildly, to hide his interest.

'Yes. Nielson went to prison for several years when the gang got broken up. Not that it changed his preferred means of dealing with people. Forrester picked up a couple of Halliwell's team. He liked having a tough guy as his foreman; liked the air of menace. It's one of the reasons I was finding it so hard to organise the workers — they were scared.'

'Okay, coming back to you.' Vaughn looked questioningly at Burns. 'I'd like to know how you ended up taking a lowly job as a machinist when you seem to be a cut above the others.'

Burns smiled. 'Don't be a snob, Inspector. No job is beneath anybody.'

'I'm not saying it is, but I strongly suspect that you're somewhat overqualified to be working here, and you're very well informed about your employers. Was there another reason why you took the job?'

'You've got me, Inspector. There was an ulterior motive, I'll admit. Nothing sinister, I can assure you.' Burns paused as if expecting Vaughn to feed him a line.

'That's for us to decide,' said Tyler, who had been silently taking notes until that point.

Vaughn was interested to see Burns's reaction. The agitator seemed pleased to have the audience participation.

'I belong to an offshoot of the TUC who are trying to engage low-paid and undervalued workers to join the unions and improve their lot.' Burns was settling into his patter now and looked completely relaxed. 'We particularly target workforces where there's a poor relationship between employers and employees.'

'So you're a mole?' Tyler interrupted.

'If you like. Don't misunderstand, though; I'm a very conscientious worker. Any employer gets his money's worth out of me.'

'But they also get more than they

bargained for,' Vaughn said wryly. 'What usually happens when they realise they've been stitched up?' An unbidden image flashed into his mind of the opened-up victim lying on a slab and Hughes poised with his needle and thread.

'I've never been found out as being anything more than a socialist who stirs things up a bit. All of the places I've worked at have had bad safety records or were known to take advantage of their workers somehow. They just needed a nudge in the right direction. I don't set up a soapbox and preach during tea breaks. I'm more subtle than that. What tends to happen is that I hand in my notice after the lads have got themselves organised — jump before I'm pushed, you might say.' Burns spread his hands. 'I'm doing nothing wrong, Inspector. Simply helping people to improve exploitative practices. And before you ask, if Forrester had started threatening me, I would just have walked away. I wouldn't have killed him. Unlike the other unlucky bastards who work here, I don't need the job.'

Too clever, too sure of himself, Vaughn thought. *Probably thinks the police are stupid.* 'Well, Mr Burns, I'll need to check your story with the local union, and I'd ask you not to move address at the moment. We may need to talk to you again.'

'Of course. I'm at your disposal. If you ask me, which you haven't, I'd say this smacks of the kind of thing the Halliwells would've done a few years ago. Maybe some of the old gang had it in for him. Ask Nielson if anyone from back then has just got out of prison.' Burns rose from his seat and sauntered out.

Vaughn let him go without a word but Tyler, as soon as the door had shut, put his notebook down and exclaimed: 'Smarmy git!'

'You can see why Nielson hates him, can't you?' Vaughn agreed. 'It doesn't make him a killer, but he's certainly suspicious.'

'But where does the doll fit into all of this, sir? It must be somehow linked with Kemp's murder. In which case, we could be wasting our time interviewing this lot.'

'It could be that this is just a copycat

killing. We'll know more when we've had a chance to examine that letter and taken a proper look at the doll. I can see that most of the ink's run, and it's in a bad condition, but I bet Hughes can make something of it. For the time being, we still have to go through all the usual motives for murder, and it looks like there were a few. Or perhaps the killer had a reason to get rid of both Kemp and Forrester.'

Vaughn rose from his chair. 'Make sure that a statement's taken from every man in the building — just the basics for now. Then we can start letting them leave. I'm going back to the station. I want to find out all we have on Nielson and see if we have anything on Burns. Maybe there'll be a link to Kemp somewhere.' He looked at his watch. 'If you get through by six, come back to the station. Otherwise you can go home.'

★　★　★

The criminal record for Gerald Henry Nielson made interesting reading. It was a wonder that he had landed himself a normal job. Vaughn would have fully expected a man with his past to be a career criminal all his life. Caught breaking and entering houses as a youngster, Nielson had progressed through smash-and-grabs to become a more shadowy character involved in organised crime — never as a leader, but often providing the muscle. Burns was right about the man's history.

The last brush with the law had come eight years ago when Nielson had been lucky to serve just two years for grievous bodily harm. The fact that Forrester had chosen to employ him as a foreman did not speak very well of his attitude to his workforce. It could also be that Forrester had some connection with the Halliwell gang that Nielson had worked for.

Vaughn had not been part of the operation to put an end to the Halliwells, but had known a lot about it as it had been the biggest bust of a criminal gang their station had ever pulled off. Wishbourne counted it as his finest hour, since he had insisted on being 'in at the kill' for the carefully orchestrated take-down.

Vaughn knew that a fair part of his colleagues' time had been taken up with keeping the chief superintendent away from any real action, but the glory had rubbed off on all of them for a while. Ron Halliwell had been sentenced to thirty-four years in total for a range of crimes, including armed robbery and murder. The turning point in the ongoing investigation had come when a former driver for the gang developed cold feet about their activities and was persuaded to become an informer.

Leafing through the reports, Vaughn found the name he half-remembered — David Evans, or Taff Evans as he was more often known. There was no recent address, but the detective inspector, Jack Taylor, who had been his contact was still very much around. Vaughn packed up the papers and returned them to their file, then went in search of Taylor.

★ ★ ★

'Taff? Yes, we're still in contact. He keeps on moaning that he misses Wales, but

69

never gets round to leaving.' Taylor took a long draught of beer. It had been late enough when Vaughn had found him that they had left the station and retired to a local pub.

Taylor was a little younger than Vaughn and liked to concentrate on organised crime rather than on the domestic murders that tended to end up at Vaughn's door.

'Did he get witness protection then?' Vaughn asked.

'As he never actually had to testify against any of the gang, we were able to keep his name out of it. He's a sly one, is our Taff. He likes to keep his options open. In the end, it looked like we'd had a lucky break when we pulled over Halliwell's car on a traffic offence and found a small fortune hidden under the engine. Taff was able to pretend he was one of the fortunate ones who escaped our sweep. He gives me occasional tips when I need them.'

'So he's still operating?'

'He says he just listens hard.' Taylor grinned. 'I have my doubts, but he's more use out there with his ear to the ground than kicking his heels in the nick.' He looked questioningly at Vaughn. 'Why do you want to know? Do you think there's a connection with the doll murders? I've been in court all day, but I heard a rumour that there are two now.'

'The second one's not a definite yet. I mean the victim's definitely dead, and there's a doll, but it could be a copycat,' Vaughn replied, feeling himself begin to relax as the alcohol got into his system. 'The victim's Malcolm Forrester.'

Taylor raised his eyebrows and whistled. 'Well, well. Forrester's dead, is he? That does surprise me.'

'What do you know about him?'

Taylor glanced around the room, but they were still the only people in The Bricklayer's Arms. 'What I know and what I suspect are two different things. I *know* that he was arrogant, heartless and completely money-driven. I *suspect* that he was peripherally involved with Halliwell and a couple of other undesirables on our books. We never had enough to even bring him in for questioning, but he floated on the edges of trouble. You're right not to just assume this is another psycho-killing. There are a lot of people who would have loved to see him dead, and this doll business has been pretty well publicised.'

'So can you ask Evans what his well-trained ears are picking up about the death? He may know about Forrester already, but the bare facts will have to be released tomorrow morning anyway, once we're sure the Forresters have all been notified.'

'The Forresters! Oh, you'll love them. Fine, upstanding citizens, every one!' Taylor's smile was wicked. 'Just make sure you take back-up. Peggy Forrester's been known to eat coppers for breakfast.'

4

A Memory from the Past

'Do you know much about Mrs Forrester, sir?' Tyler asked curiously. The house they had pulled up outside of was substantial but not in the better part of the city.

'Only a bit,' Vaughn answered noncommittally. In fact, Detective Inspector Taylor had said quite a lot, none of it complementary. He rang the doorbell, and the door was presently opened by a stocky woman who glared at them from red-rimmed eyes.

'Police?' she barked.

'Detective Inspector Vaughn, and this is Detective Sergeant Tyler,' Vaughn announced. 'May we come in?'

Saying nothing, the woman walked back into the house, leaving the door open for them to follow her. She entered the kitchen and sat down at the table.

'Make yourselves comfortable. I've got a fair few questions for you,' she said.

'I'm very sorry to meet you under such sad circumstances, Mrs Forrester.'

'Can it. I'm not interested in fake sympathy. You lot tried to get Malcolm on a load of trumped-up charges a few years ago. I ought to throw you out of the house, but I want to find out who murdered him.' Peggy Forrester leaned forward, looking intently at Vaughn. 'Gerry Nielson came round last night to pay his respects. Unlike you, he actually cares. According to him, there's some commie bastard who had it in for Malcolm. Is that right?'

Vaughn thought quickly. They had not intended to release the information that Forrester was probably the second victim of a serial killer, but he had to head off any personal vendetta that a woman like Peggy Forrester could start. With her contacts, Burns would be a marked man. 'I'm afraid that Mr Nielson was not in possession of all the facts about your husband's death.' He briefly explained about the discovery of the doll, momentarily stunning his listener.

'You mean it could be some psycho?' Peggy asked incredulously.

'The early signs are that the two murders were committed by the same person,' Vaughn answered cautiously. 'Did you know Keith Kemp, the first victim?' He passed her the photograph of Kemp to study.

'I'd certainly never heard the name before it was in the papers.' Peggy peered at the photograph, then cursed and took a pair of glasses out of a drawer. 'No, never seen him before.'

The belligerence had been knocked out of her and for the first time she looked vulnerable. 'I was sure, when I heard about Malcolm, that one of his old enemies had finally done him in. I'll admit he had a few. But they wouldn't go in for this kind of sick joke.'

'It would be helpful anyway to have a list of the people you suspected. Someone chose Mr Forrester for a reason, and until we're sure of that reason, I want all the information I can get.' Vaughn leaned forward, echoing her belligerent pose from earlier. He pointed a warning finger at her. 'What I don't want is any personal investigations going on behind my back.'

Peggy returned his stare defiantly but finally pursed her lips and nodded. 'All right, I get the picture. I won't go barging in just yet. But you'd better get results. I *will* get justice for Malcolm, one way or another.' She turned her attention to Tyler. 'You got your pencil ready? These are the men who hated Malcolm enough to top him.' She reeled off six names, many of whom rang a bell with the two detectives. 'If any of them have some weird fetish about dolls, then you've got your man. But if it's just some nutter, then God knows how you'll catch him.'

Privately sharing her opinion, Vaughn moved on to more mundane but important questions. Forrester had left the house at six o'clock yesterday morning, heading for his factory. He liked to get in early some mornings and shout at anyone who turned up late. Other times he would saunter in at lunch time or not at all. Keep them guessing seemed to have been his approach. Peggy confirmed that Forrester had trusted Nielson with most of the day-to-day work while he drummed up orders and took care of the business side. When asked about their sons, Peggy said that they had their own jobs, one in shipping and one running a pub in the city centre.

'So, will they inherit the factory?' Vaughn asked, thinking of motive once again.

'No. Malcolm always said the lads had to make their own fortunes. I'll be running the place from now on.' There was a slight satisfaction in her voice. 'I already do the books, and if those lazy sods think they can get anything past me, they'll have to think again.'

Vaughn mentally moved Peggy Forrester up the list of possible suspects. Although his instincts told him she had not killed her husband, she had gained a free hand in a very profitable business. Perhaps her husband had been cheating on her. Vaughn uncharitably thought it quite likely, taking in her stony features and lumpen figure. The doll, however, was the sticking point. It was totally out of place in that kind of domestic killing.

Considering the wildly different personalities and lives of Kemp and Forrester as he drove away from the house, Vaughn was becoming sure that the dolls would prove to be the key to it all.

* * *

When Vaughn arrived back in his office, there was a note from Wishbourne asking for an update as soon as he returned. He considered it for a moment and then dropped it behind the radiator. If asked, he would say it must have blown off his desk. He did not need a grilling from the superintendent right now. What he needed was to find out more about the dolls. He had already sent Tyler off to check through the names on Peggy Forester's list, but he would follow a different line of enquiry. Leafing through his notes, he found the telephone number for Humphrey Grace.

'Sorry to disturb you again, Mr Grace. It's Detective Inspector Vaughn.'

'Hello! It's no trouble, I do assure you,' the reply came back. 'I was going to call you anyway. Now, I don't want to get your hopes up, but I may have found a lead for you on that doll.'

'That would be most helpful,' Vaughn said, his spirits beginning to rise.

'I thought there was something familiar about it. I have of course seen several dolls of that kind, but there was something about that *particular* one that stirred a vague memory. I've been taxing my mind with it and I finally remembered. When I was a young man, I worked in Austria for a little over a year, learning the European trade and improving my languages. I became good friends with one of the other apprentices in the business, a man named Hans Kugelbreck. One day he came back from a meeting with a client and told me about a collection of dolls that had struck him as being very interesting. He described one in great detail as it reminded him of his uncle. It was very smartly dressed in a black suit and had a silver tie-pin with a fox's head. Beautiful miniature work, so

Kugelbreck said, and so lifelike. He felt that the maker must have been copying from a real model to get the look on the doll's face.'

'A silver tie-pin? That's just like our doll!' Vaughn exclaimed.

'Exactly. I can see it quite clearly on the photograph.' Grace was excited.

'Can we get in touch with Mr Kugelbreck, see if he can confirm this?'

'Ah, this is where it gets a little problematic. He retired a few years ago and moved out of Vienna to somewhere in the countryside. I don't have an address for him, but I'm sure we can track him down, Inspector,' Grace assured Vaughn. 'He's an expert in Dutch art, particularly eighteenth-century. Our business pays little heed to claims that people have stopped working. I myself have officially retired twice already. His auction house will know how to contact him.'

Vaughn let out a sigh of relief. To get such a good lead and see it peter out would have been a blow. 'You've been a great help. I'm very grateful. If you can give me the number for Mr Kugelbreck's former employers, we can take it from here.'

'Of course. Kugelbreck speaks excellent English, so you won't need an interpreter, and I expect that the staff at the auction house will too. Or perhaps you speak German yourself?'

'Not really,' Vaughn replied awkwardly. Languages had not played a big part in his police career, and he had forgotten most of the little French and German he had been taught at school.

'Not to worry. If you encounter any problems you're most welcome to call on me. I'm happy to help.' Grace's voice grew more serious. 'This business is rather unpleasant and reflects badly on people who truly appreciate toys as works of art.'

'We're doing our utmost to end this case, I do assure you.'

'Yes, but what if it's part of something bigger?' Grace pressed. 'I'd be afraid to sell such a doll at the moment. I'd be wondering if it was intended for a very dark purpose.'

Given the fact that news had not yet

got out that a second doll-related death had occurred, Vaughn thought that Grace was uncannily prescient. He thanked the elderly expert once again and finished the call. It was only eleven o'clock, and the time difference between Britain and Austria was small, so they would still be well within working hours. Vaughn spent a few minutes dredging up the German phrase he wanted and then dialled the number Grace had provided. When a female voice answered, he managed to say, '*Guten tag. Sprechen Sie Englisch?*'

'Yes, sir. How can I help you?' came the receptionist's reply.

'Good. I would like to contact Herr Hans Kugelbreck. Mr Humphrey Grace told me that you could help?'

'Oh, we can always help a friend of Humphrey's. If you'd wait just a moment.' The receptionist quickly found an address and telephone number for Kugelbreck. 'Herr Kugelbreck is usually at home in the evenings, and he won't mind being telephoned if it's about business.'

'Actually, it's his specialist knowledge that I'm after. Well, thank you.' Vaughn rang off. Armed with something good to report at last, he sent for Tyler and took the sergeant with him to report to Chief Superintendent Wishbourne.

* * *

Wishbourne grunted when Vaughn and Tyler entered his office. 'Another murder, another doll. No suspects, no witnesses, no leads. This is starting to look very bad for us, gentlemen!' He hammered a meaty fist on his desk. 'I want results, and I want them now!'

'Actually, I think we may finally have a lead to follow, sir,' Vaughn said when the chief superintendent paused for breath.

'Then tell me!' Wishbourne demanded.

'The doll that was left beside Kemp has been provisionally identified by one of the British experts we consulted. I'm hoping to talk to an Austrian expert this afternoon to confirm this. We can send photographs of both dolls by airmail to this man, but I can certainly describe them in detail over the phone.'

'I'd far rather have an imminent arrest

than an identification of those blasted dolls!' Wishbourne exclaimed. 'Surely we can bring some people in for questioning in relation to the second murder. Forrester knew too many criminals for his own good.'

'Sergeant Tyler has been investigating all the possible associates that Mrs Forrester and Inspector Jack Taylor have suggested. There seems to be genuine bafflement about the death. I'm convinced that the dolls themselves have more to tell us.'

'Well you're not calling in a bloody ventriloquist!' Wishbourne exclaimed, venting his frustration on his officers.

'One person I think we should call in is a criminal psychologist,' Vaughn answered calmly. 'This is stranger than most murders we encounter, and he might be able to help.'

'A sensible suggestion at last. Okay, I can authorise that.' The chief superintendent began to calm down. 'If you think you're on to something with this expert, we should be able to get pictures to Austria more quickly if we use the

Foreign Office. I attended a dinner where mention was made of better ways to send pictures down a telephone wire. Damned if I know how, but I can probably sort out a contact at the British Embassy in Vienna for you.'

'That would make a big difference, sir,' Vaughn said gratefully.

'Let me know how the phone conversation goes. As for you, Tyler, keep on digging into Forrester's life. I don't want us to miss anything.'

'Yes, sir,' Tyler replied. 'I've set up a meeting with an informant, David Evans, who knows all about that side of things.'

'Get on with it then — both of you. I'll be waiting for your reports.'

Outside the office, Tyler rolled his eyes. 'Have it done yesterday, as usual,' he summed up the chief superintendent's approach.

'He has a point,' Vaughn said. 'I don't expect you to find much out from Taff Evans, but you never know. Where are you meeting him?'

'DI Taylor suggested a pub near Evans's flat. It's not too far.'

'Okay, come and see me as soon as you get back. We'll tackle Wishbourne together.'

'Sounds good to me,' Tyler said, and set off to his rendezvous.

Vaughn had briefly thought about going with him, but it should be an easy interview; the man either did or did not have information for them. He checked in with two of the officers who were helping to sift through the statements given by all of Forrester's employees, but as yet they had found nothing out of the ordinary. It was annoying that the factory was rather out of the way. The murderer had got into the building somehow or other and no one had seen him do it. Or her, he corrected himself. He was assuming the killer was a man, but they had no evidence either way.

The agitator, Burns, had checked out with the local union representative, and they had admitted to encouraging his activities. He had handed in his notice and was lying low — probably a wise move, considering how much the fore-man, Nielson, hated him.

Still thinking about the layout of the factory, Vaughn went in search of Hughes. He needed some more information about Forrester's death. 'Tom, have you got a minute?' he said, peering round the door to the pathologist's office.

'Come in. I'm expecting a body to turn up shortly but I'm free until then,' Hughes replied.

'Nothing related to my case, I hope?'

'It's an exhumation actually. There's been a hint that someone's death was not natural after all.'

'Exhumation! How old is the corpse?' Vaughn asked with some level of interest.

'Only a few weeks, but you still might want to be gone by the time it arrives. It won't be pleasant.'

'About Forrester.' Vaughn got straight to the point. 'Do you have a definitive report for me?'

'It's being typed up at the moment. Nothing new to add really. He was hit hard on the back of the head with something like a hammer. This killed him before he was left in the water, as there were no signs of drowning. He died between five in the morning and noon.'

'And as we now know that he is said to have left home at six, and the factory workers arrived at eight, we can say with some certainty that he was killed between six-thirty and eight,' Vaughn added.

'That's right. Not very helpful I'm afraid. We didn't find anything amiss in the room, or on Forrester. No prints at all on the doll. Just like the other one. I wish I could give you more, but that's all there is.'

'Did you ever handle a body that was a victim of the Anderson gang?' Vaughn asked.

Hughes thought for a moment. 'Yes, I believe I did. A young man who had been killed for stealing from one of their lock-ups.'

'Any similarities?'

'Now you're clutching at straws!' Hughes smiled wryly. 'I know a bit about the Andersons' habits and I don't think any of them would have come up with the doll idea. It's just not their style. Most of them are still in prison anyway.'

'I think that's a dead end too, but you

never know,' Vaughn agreed. 'We can't seem to find any connection between the two corpses other than their deaths.'

'And the fact that they lived in Manchester.'

'Well, yes, but so do a lot of people.'

'Bear with me, Greg,' Hughes said, flicking out a notebook and picking up a pen. 'Let's list the similarities. One — both male and within ten years of each other. Two — both lived in Manchester. Three — both found with a doll that closely resembles them. Now for the differences. Kemp lived alone, apparently blamelessly, and there seems to have been no reason to kill him. Forrester, on the other hand, had a family and contacts that made the Krays look like choirboys. There are several possible motives for *his* death, but none that spring to mind for the *particular* means of his death.'

'What if Kemp was killed by a madman but Forrester by a known associate who's trying to make it look like another doll killing?'

Hughes shook his head. 'There weren't that many details released about the doll.

It's inconceivable that a copycat killer could have got hold of such a good match for the first doll that also looked like Forrester. Besides . . . there's the letters.'

'How about this, then?' Vaughn said, leaning his weight against the wall. 'The killer wants to do away with Forrester for personal reasons and hits on the idea of hiding his crime under the 'mad serial killer' banner. It's been done before. Perhaps he's seen a doll that looks like Forrester and got the idea for it. Then Kemp would've been killed as a diversion.' He grimaced at Hughes's raised eyebrows and shook his head. 'No, I don't believe that either. It's too far-fetched.'

'Much too far-fetched,' agreed Hughes. 'I can't say that it's impossible, because patently it *could* have happened that way, but I don't think it did. There are far easier ways to have killed Forrester and got away with it. I could think of several myself.'

'You know, I sometimes wonder if I could think of a way to commit the perfect murder.'

'Have you ever come up with one?'

Hughes asked, a slight smile on his face.

'Not yet. Which is strange, as I've certainly known of some unsolved cases. But I think the killers who've evaded capture were lucky more than anything else. I can't think of anything particularly clever about their crimes.'

'Well, I don't know if this killer is clever or just cracked, but we're the ones who need the luck at the moment.'

★　★　★

Tyler had been unimpressed by Taff Evans. Reporting back to Vaughn, he talked disparagingly of Evans being the most boring man he had ever met. 'I mean, when you think of a grass, you imagine someone scrawny, probably hanging around the back of a pub with a cigarette looking nervous. Evans, on the other hand, is fat and balding. I know from DI Taylor that he used to be in with the wrong crowd, and you'd think he'd have some decent stories to tell, but he's just like an old slug. All he does is sit there sponging pints off folk.'

'You've been watching too much TV,' Vaughn retorted, amused by his sergeant's naivety. 'It's of no interest to us what a grass looks like, although I will grant you that I've met a few that match the stereotype. What matters is what they know.'

'Precious little, in this case!' Tyler opened his notebook. 'He heard about Forrester's death by the end of the day we found him. Word travelled fast. According to Evans, the 'jungle drums were beating double time' because of Forrester's association with undesirables. No one has started bragging about taking him out, and Evans doesn't know of any current grudges that would lead to murder. In fact, he said that the usual suspects are all a bit creeped out by the way Forrester was killed; you know, the doll connection. It's got a lot of the tough guys worried.'

'I can understand that. Those types have a certain acceptance that they might be attacked for their actions, but the thought of one of them being killed almost randomly by some maniac is something they wouldn't expect.'

'You've put it better than Evans, but yes, that was his thought too.'

'So he had nothing for us?' Vaughn asked with resignation.

'Nothing about the killer, but he did say that he wouldn't be surprised if the family go looking for revenge.'

Vaughn nodded. 'I'm just glad that Mrs Forrester has held off for a bit to let us find him.'

'According to Evans, it's the eldest son, Joe, that's the problem. He runs a pub where far too many of the old faces turn up, and he's got a foul temper, just like his parents.' Tyler checked his notebook. 'It's The Crown on Balmoral Street.'

'I know it. A complete dive that attracts the worst of the worst.' Vaughn rose from his chair and took his coat down from a hanger. 'Still, I could do with a drink, so maybe we should go and check out this Joe Forrester. If only to warn him off the investigation.'

★　★　★

'That's Joe over there by the pool table.' A grossly fat man with stubbled jowls and tattoos jabbed a thumb towards the rear of the pub before sullenly returning to his beer.

'Thanks.' Vaughn nodded to his sergeant and the two walked over to where four men were taking it in turns to play pool. 'I'm looking for Joe Forrester.'

Four faces that could not be described as handsome turned as one.

'I'm Joe. Who are you?' enquired a wiry skinhead. The grip on his pool cue tightened, and it was obvious he was ready to use it for a purpose other than that for which it had been intended.

'Detective Inspector Vaughn.'

With a sneer, Forrester weighed up the two policemen, his piggy eyes narrowing. 'What do you want? If this is about my dad's death, then I've got only one thing to say.'

'And what's that?' Vaughn asked.

'You'd better get to whoever did it before I do.'

'I'm here to warn you to stay out of this. Let us do the investigating.' Vaughn could detect movement behind him and he was aware that some of the other figures he had seen in the pub were crowding around. Police or not, one step out of line here and things could turn very nasty.

Forrester spat derisively on the floor. 'Mum said we were to give you a chance, but I'm not sure I agree. Not now I've seen you.'

'Take your mum's advice, son,' said Vaughn patronisingly, noting the angry twitch of the man's face. 'You don't have the resources or the information we do, and you certainly don't have the authority. If I find you've been meddling, I'll be down on you like a ton of bricks.' Warning given, he turned, and with Tyler at his heels left the pub.

5

The Third Doll

The next death linked to the ongoing investigation was as grisly as it was public.

The unfortunate victim was discovered impaled by an eight-foot-long four-inch-diameter scaffolding tube on a side street just off one of the main roads in the town, the bizarre sight attracting many ghoulish onlookers. And whilst most — if not all — assumed it to be nothing more than a freak accident, the presence of the similarly impaled doll lying close to the deceased suggested otherwise. At its feet rested the now-familiar brown envelope.

The police had set up a cordon blocking off both ends of the street when Vaughn arrived on the scene. A large sheet of white tarpaulin was being set up to shield the police activity from the morbidly curious.

'I've little doubt that death would have

been more or less instantaneous,' said Hughes, who had got there with Tyler ten minutes earlier. 'The poor fellow wouldn't have known what hit him.'

Vaughn turned his gaze to the forty-five-foot-high scaffolding structure that had been erected to facilitate the repair work being done to a large building. To his admittedly untrained eye, it all looked safe and secure.

'Looking at the position of the body,' Hughes commented, 'I'd say that the victim passed along the walkway under the scaffolding, and it was once he stepped from underneath that the killer struck. Given the fact that the metal pole has punched straight through the shoulder, running the length of the man's torso and part of his right leg, exiting at the ankle, I think it's reasonable to assume that it was dropped from the very top of the scaffolding.'

'Christ! I've seen it all now!' Vaughn commented. 'Surely someone else must have been around, even though it's early. Any witnesses?' His question was levelled at Tyler.

'Not as yet, sir. Clearly whoever did this chose their moment precisely. It's a bit of a back alley round this side, and I'd guess there aren't many people who come down here. From the briefcase, I'd say the victim was on his way to work.'

'Do we have an ID yet?'

'Just waiting for the photographer, then I'll check his pockets.'

Vaughn nodded and turned his attention reluctantly to the dark-suited, bowler-hatted corpse which, due to the rigidity of the metal pole, was propped obscenely in a shop doorway. The blood had got to the sticky stage and lay slick on the pavement. The face was undamaged, and Vaughn guessed the man had been nearing retirement age. He could see a wedding ring on one hand, and the clothes were of good quality, only slightly worn. Whatever kind of job the victim had been going to must pay well. He turned away from the body — it could tell him no more at present, and he crouched down to appraise the doll.

Like a piece of kebabbed meat, it too had been run through by a metal skewer of a kind he had seen in butchers' shops, and it too wore a bowler hat. The face was recognisable as being painted in a very similar fashion to the other two dolls. The delicate brushstrokes that made up the eyebrows were particularly characteristic. The features were quite individual and depicted an older man, somewhat digni- fied in appearance, with wrinkles on his forehead and heavy lines at the sides of his mouth. Its clothes were similar to the victim's — a black suit with a miniature pocket-watch and chain looped across the waistcoat. Vaughn used a pen to gently push at the small hat but was unsurprised to find that it was attached to the head.

'Mike's here,' announced Tyler, step- ping to one side to allow the police photographer to begin taking some snapshots.

'Good.' Vaughn greeted the photogra- pher and moved away, turning his gaze to the top of the scaffold tower where the killer had no doubt been skulking. He passed under the walkway, to where a ladder permitted access to the top and began to ascend. Despite having a fairly strong fear of heights, and the fact that the ladder was somewhat rickety, he made it to the top, exiting onto a vertiginous gantry that spanned the rooftops. Sundry work tools — hammers, saws, chisels, coils of rope and empty buckets — lay scattered haphazardly on the wooden framework, and the boards creaked ominously as Vaughn shuffled warily along to the far end where several more scaffolding tubes lay.

'Do you want me to come up, sir?' Tyler cried.

Like a condemned pirate, Vaughn made his slow, fear-laden way to the edge of the planking and gazed over the rim. He gulped as he looked down, half-expecting to see circling dorsal fins, and for a moment his head swam. 'No. I . . . I'm all right. I'll just take a look around up here.' Stepping backwards over a small heap of bricks, he began to search for anything of importance. Now that his initial fear of falling, or for the whole structure to collapse about him, had gone, he noticed that there was a small square opening — no doubt at one time a window aperture — at the opposite end, near to where the ladder rested. Clambering over, he looked inside and saw a cluttered room. On the dusty floorboards, leading to an open door, was a trail of footprints. Knowing that he risked contaminating this 'evidence' if he were to enter, he climbed back down the ladder.

After the impaled corpse had been photographed from numerous different angles, Tyler searched it. From the personal effects and the material contained in the briefcase, the identity of the victim was established — Mr Simon Willoughby, barrister for one of the biggest legal firms in the city.

'Now comes the nasty part,' announced Hughes. Together with Lockwood and another of his assistants, a chubby man named Paul Havers, they lowered the corpse to the ground and proceeded to extricate the metal pole. It was messy work and Vaughn was forced to look away.

'I suppose they have to do that in order to get the poor bugger into the ambulance,' said Tyler. Wincing with revulsion, he watched the gruesome spectacle.

'I want this whole area searched before the clean-up crew arrive,' said Vaughn. 'There's a room in the adjoining building that the killer could well have used as an escape route. There are definitely footprints, and we should check for fingerprints as well. I'd like a map of any other exit and entry points so that they can be searched too.' He scratched his head. 'Get some uniformed officers in and get as many statements as you can. I don't see how something as public as this could've gone unnoticed. Someone must've seen something. Ask the shopkeepers, the postmen. Find out about the building company.' He turned, ready to go, then stopped. 'You know, Wishbourne's going to go ballistic over this.'

★   ★   ★

'Three down. Three to go.'

Absently, Vaughn looked down at the scribbled note, his mind going over the lambasting he had just received from his superior. As grillings went, this had been one of the harshest of his career thus far. He dreaded to think what was going to happen if the killer were to complete his quota of murders before they got to him. He found himself reflecting that if that were to happen, he could well be given his marching orders; pensioned off into an early retirement. And whilst some may have welcomed such a move, it was a prospect that did not sit comfortably with him.

The door opened and Tyler entered. 'Sir, good news. We may have found a witness to this morning's event.'

Vaughn's eyes widened. 'Oh?'

'Yes.' The detective sergeant paused for a moment. 'Believe it or not, it's Wilkes's uncle.'

'Not Andy Wilkes? Christ, everyone knows he's the biggest piss artist in the area. He's been a drunk ever since getting kicked out of the army. I remember hearing a rumour that he was experimented on at Porton Down — that they subjected him to nerve gas or something. Completely messed him up. Made him as mad as a March hare.'

'I don't know about that, sir. Suffice to say that he's waiting outside. And I mean *outside*. Considering his stink, it was thought better for him not to enter the station.'

Reluctantly, Vaughn rose from his chair. 'All right. Let's see what he's got to say.'

Both detectives left the office and proceeded to the station exit, aware of a growing odour. There, sat outside on a low bench, was a raggedly bearded figure of indeterminate age. In one hand he clutched a plastic carrier bag no doubt filled with scraps scavenged from back alleys and waste bins. From the filthy clothes — the knee-length shabby coat that was soiled with dirt and the ratty bobble hat — it was blatantly obvious that the man was a tramp. The large coat was smeared in caked excrement and hung open at the front, revealing a ripped string vest and a pair of obscenely stained blue underpants. His legs were white and skinny, the exposed flesh covered in sores and bruises. On his feet he wore a pair of damp red slippers from which his scabrous toes and hideously twisted toenails protruded. He had the appearance of someone who had just crawled from a sewer.

Catching Vaughn's disapproving stare, the man hiccoughed and gave a salute with a hand caked in grime. He belched and wafted aside the fouled air before unsteadily getting to his feet. 'Why, if it isn't my old friend Inspector Vaughn,' he said, his words slurred, his voice harsh and gravelly. There was no pleasantry in the man's words, just bitterness and venom. Hawking back a wad of phlegm, the tramp spat and dropped the bag which contained his worldly possessions on the ground. He reached into a pocket of his coat, removed an open can of lager and raised it to his cracked lips, sucking on it with the eagerness of a starving calf at its mother's udder. He gave an unsteady backwards lurch, regained his balance and staggered forward a step. For a moment it looked as though he was going to be sick.

'Hello, Andy. I understand that you've some information that may be of interest.' Despite trying to remain cordial, Vaughn's stare hardened. Under different conditions he might have felt some sympathy for this poor wretch; but having just endured Wishbourne's severe dressing-down, he was not in the mood. He stepped back, distancing himself from his unwanted informant. The reek was making his eyes water. Despite the overall level of unpleasantness of his situation, there was a certain something about the man that drew his curiosity. He had seen homeless people aplenty, and there were some he saw regularly, either slumming it in cardboard boxes in shop doorways or curled up in bus shelters; but he was seldom this close to one, and from a purely sociological perspective it was interesting to see just how low a man could sink.

Draining his can dry, Andy then crushed it in his fist. He lowered his head, staring at the ground at his feet. 'I saw him,' he mumbled.

Vaughn stiffened. 'Sorry?'

'I said, I saw him,' Wilkes repeated, his eyes still cast downward.

'Who? Who did you see?'

'Death.' Wilkes raised his face, his eyes bloodshot. 'It was Death, I tell you. He walked right past me, his face all pale and . . . and . . . whiter than chalk, like it was a mask. There was a dead look to him. Blank, like a skull almost . . . and he was dressed in a long black hooded cloak.'

'I see,' Vaughn muttered. 'And I suppose he carried a pitchfork as well?'

'That's the Devil, sir,' Tyler corrected. 'Death carries a scythe. You know, as in the Grim Reaper.'

'That's it! The Grim Reaper! That's who I saw.' Wilkes began to tremble. 'He stopped and stared over to where I sat huddled in the shadows, and that look chilled me to the bone. But I don't think he actually saw me.'

Shaking his head disparagingly, Vaughn looked away to one side for a moment, vaguely taking in the relatively sane brickwork of the police station foreground. There was little doubt in his mind that Wilkes's witness account was fuelled by excess alcohol consumption and that they were just wasting their time.

Certainly things were bad, but they were not quite bad enough to rely on the drunken ramblings of this sorry wretch.

'I saw him, I tell you. He was as real as you standing there,' Wilkes blurted. 'And then he strode past me, and crept out of the opening and out on to the scaffolding. He had something clutched tight to his body . . . a doll, I think. And he was speaking to it; cursing it.'

* * *

Dr Ralph Coleman was a tall, thin-faced man with large owlish eyes like those of Marty Feldman. He walked stooped, his long arms behind his back, hands clasped together as though he was carrying an invisible load; and his brow was constantly furrowed, as if he was either in pain or in deep thought. In most cases it was the latter, for he was a criminal psychologist — one of the best, and the conundrum that had been presented to him was one that was as perplexing as it was disturbing.

'Well, those are the facts of the case so

far,' Vaughn prompted, having watched Coleman in silence for the past minute or so. He was becoming annoyed with the other's continuous pacing. 'Is there anything you can tell me that'll be of assistance? Some hint as to the personality of the culprit that we can be on the lookout for?'

Coleman came to an abrupt stop. He turned to face the detective. 'Personality wise, I think the first thing to say is that this is a truly disturbed individual. I'd hedge my bets that it's a male, under fifty, and someone with deeply rooted psychological problems. Problems that have been festering for a long time, quite probably since childhood.' Taking his chair, the psychologist glanced briefly at his notes. 'As far as the dolls are concerned, I'm of the firm opinion that they don't represent 'calling cards'. At least, not in terms of usual criminal terminology such as those employed by Jack the Ripper or the Zodiac Killer, where the focus was on taunting the police and obliquely claiming responsibility. Rather, they signify something far more intrinsic. It's quite possible that, to the murderer, each doll represents a facet of themselves; an inner demon, if you like — something which is loathed and feared and has to be destroyed. The fact that the dolls bear a strong resemblance to the victim is most fascinating, yet not that surprising.'

'In what way?' Vaughn asked interestedly.

'No doubt you're aware of voodoo dolls and the manner in which they are made to duplicate the intended victim? These dolls, or puppets, may be fashioned from such materials as a carved root, grain or corn shafts, fruit, paper, wax, a potato, clay, branches, or cloth stuffed with herbs, with the intent that any actions performed upon the effigy will be transferred to the subject based on sympathetic magic.'

Vaughn nodded.

'Well, it's possible that what we have here is a sort of voodoo in reverse; a mirror-image almost.'

'You've lost me, I'm afraid,' Vaughn admitted.

'Let me try and explain.' Coleman pondered for a moment. 'Imagine yourself in the mind of our killer. Now let's assume that, somehow, probably against your will, you've come into possession of a number of antique dolls of varying appearance; dolls which, due to your entrenched phobias, you consider malign; alien even.' He pointed directly at the detective. 'What would you do?'

'Why . . . get rid of them, of course.'

'Exactly. But what if you couldn't? What if each time you tried to dispose of them or destroy them, you found that they returned?'

'I guess I'd be forced to question my sanity. But surely, if you were to chop them up or burn them, give them away or throw them in the bin — ?'

Coleman interrupted by wagging a finger. 'Ah, but remember, our murderer doesn't think along such lines of rationality. In his mind, he may well *believe* that he's done so, whereas in reality he's done nothing of the sort. It's a well-known phenomenon; a mental deception almost. One only has to think of the numerous

111

accounts of so-called cursed items that form an unbreakable negative attachment, which abound in many myths and legends from all over the world. Now let's take this a step further and imagine that this has been going on for months, even years, until . . . until a time when a true means of unburdening himself of the 'curse', for lack of a better word, is discovered.'

'And what would that be?'

'It's my belief that our murderer thinks he can rid himself of the doll, or rather dolls, by killing what he sees as their human doppelgänger. In his eyes, someone who bears a likeness to the doll *becomes* the doll, and once that person is murdered then the doll, too, is murdered in a similar fashion. Potential victims become objectified. Expunged of human traits, they become easier to exterminate. In short, only by killing the doll's living doppelgänger is our killer capable of finally 'killing' the doll. And, in my view, that's the motive behind these deaths. Warped, undoubtedly . . . but given the details, the best conclusion I can reach.

As with voodoo, I think it's also important that the doll is ritually slaughtered in a similar manner to the deceased. Take the Kemp doll, for instance — if Kemp had been shot or stabbed to death, then the doll would bear similar injuries. It is inconceivable to imagine that the doll is 'killed' first and that its human doppelgänger is then slain in the same manner.'

Vaughn leaned forward in his chair. 'So let me get this straight. The killer kills people who look like his dolls in order to 'free' himself of their . . . possession?'

'Exactly. I would think that he must be of an extremely obsessive disposition. An avid person-watcher; a borderline voyeur. Someone who spies a lot and who frequents places where he can observe surreptitiously. I wouldn't like to guess how long it's taken for this person to track down lookalikes, but I'd assume it's been a long time. Now I think the wait is over and he's putting his plan into practice. Another thing of significance is the fact that the killer, certainly from his actions, seems to be constrained to certain principles in relation to how he carries out each murder. Take, for instance, the fact that he goes to such elaborate lengths as dropping a metal scaffolding pole from a height. Wouldn't it be easier and far more likely to guarantee success to just walk up behind someone and shoot them?'

'And without knowing what the remaining dolls look like, no one is safe,' Vaughn added.

'I'm afraid so.'

'What about our sole witness account — the possibility that the killer dresses as Death?'

'If it's accurate, then it's perhaps but another facet of his madness.' Coleman gathered his papers together and placed them in a folder. 'Well, as insane as it undoubtedly sounds, that's the best I can offer at the moment. Obviously if new evidence comes to light, I may have to review my theory.' He got to his feet. 'Be sure and let me know if there are any further developments.'

Vaughn nodded. His mind was a turmoil of thoughts and ideas as he tried

to comprehend what he had just been told.

⋆ ⋆ ⋆

'You're not buying into this rubbish, are you, sir?' inquired Tyler after he had been informed of his superior's discussion with Coleman. 'I mean, let's face it — it's pretty far-fetched, don't you think?'

Vaughn sipped from his coffee. It was now late afternoon and it would soon be time to head home.

'I can just imagine what old Wishbourne's going to say if you tell him,' Tyler added. 'Death prowling the streets dropping scaffolding poles on people, and voodoo dolls. Hell, he'll go nuts!'

'Maybe, maybe not. Anyway, Coleman's the expert. He knows what he's talking about, and I've no reason to challenge his theories. Besides, as there's virtually nothing else to go on, I don't see why we shouldn't go along with what he says. Yes, I'd be the first to admit it's weird, but so's everything concerning this bloody case. I mean, let's face it, the only

115

connection between the three victims that we've as yet established lies with the dolls. The key to solving this and finding the killer has to be there, somewhere.'

'We'll get the bastard, sir. It's just a matter of time. Who knows, maybe he'll make a slip-up. After all, if Coleman's right with his profiling, then it sounds to me that the killer's quite a risk-taker. That stands to reason.'

'Why do you say that?' Vaughn asked.

'Well I think he got lucky, certainly with Kemp and Willoughby. With Kemp, I wonder what would've happened if he hadn't forced the car off the road. What if Kemp hadn't swerved? Same with Willoughby. What if he'd missed with the scaffolding pipe . . . or only wounded his target? All that waiting, watching and planning up in smoke.'

'I hadn't thought of that.' Vaughn finished his coffee, then got to his feet. 'You know, it scares me sometimes when I stop and think that somewhere out there, there's a complete and utter nutcase walking around; and what's more, he could be anyone. Just as his victims could be almost anyone. Who knows, there could be a doll out there that looks just like you . . . or me. There's a comforting thought for you.'

6

Blood on the Altar

Two days had passed since Simon Willoughby had been found pinned to the pavement, and Vaughn and his team were no nearer apprehending his murderer. Well aware that it was not a question of *if* but rather *when* the killer would strike again, there had been a heightened police presence on the city streets. Yet Vaughn was only too well aware that there was a limit to what public protection the police could provide; and the disturbing thought — indeed, the reality of the situation — was that all were currently at the mercy of the murderer.

Unsurprisingly, there was now widespread media coverage, the death of Willoughby acting as the catalyst for a whole deluge of sensationalist reporting and scaremongering. And while the released details were vague and sketchy, there was enough printed in the newspapers and broadcast on television and radio to engender an almost pervasive sense of paranoia. Few were comfortable knowing that there was a madman on the loose — a psychopath who, as far as most were aware, targeted his victims at random, and for whom life was simply there for the taking.

'At least the papers haven't got wind of the killer going around dressed as Death yet,' commented Tyler, having just flicked through a copy of the morning *Standard*. 'God alone knows what they'd make of that.'

'It's only a matter of time.' Vaughn stubbed out a cigarette. 'We've been lucky so far that none of these bloody reporters has found out about the details of the letter. They know there was an envelope, but fortunately the contents haven't been disclosed. Can you imagine what they'd do if they heard there were a further three on the hit-list?'

Tyler nodded.

In a sudden burst of anger, Vaughn thumped a fist hard against his desk. 'It's getting to me, knowing that all we're doing is sitting around waiting for this bastard to kill again. I can picture him laughing at us, gleefully running rings around us. He knows he's got the upper hand and that he's free to strike at leisure.' In frustration, he snapped a pen.

'That's not quite true, now is it, sir? I mean it might sound contradictory, but I think he's both a planner and an opportunist, certainly in the case of Willoughby, and I'd suggest Kemp as well. What gets me is, where the hell does he find his victims? Does he sit in the market square keeping an eye on everyone? Scoping passers-by; looking them over for characteristic facial warts, moustaches and haircuts?'

Vaughn shrugged his shoulders. 'Your guess is as good as mine.' For some reason he wanted to be alone, to think things through in the solitude of his office. 'Why don't you go and see if either Hughes or Lockwood have anything new? Report back to me later.' He watched as his somewhat disgruntled sergeant left the office, then lit another cigarette. He got to his feet and went over to the window, noting the specimen box in which the three dolls retrieved thus far were currently stored, having been brought in earlier by Tyler from the evidence room. From outside the police station came the familiar warble of a squad car's siren.

Vaughn picked up the box and returned to his desk. Removing the dolls, he studied them carefully. The workmanship was obvious, even to him. From the carefully painted faces to the exquisitely made clothing, they were painstakingly detailed. The Forrester doll, as he thought of it, was still a little damp from its time in the tank. He checked each layer of clothing on the dolls, and the porcelain hands and feet, but found no marks. The bodies were made of densely packed cloth rather than porcelain — or bisque, as he believed the experts called it. The eyes were made of glass and were rather unsettling: evil in a way he was unable to fully comprehend.

Turning over the Forrester doll, the detective noted the section on the back of its head which had been cracked. Filled with a sense of revulsion, he put the doll back on the table and turned away.

It was a little early, but Vaughn decided to try Kugelbreck's number again, for there had been no reply on the previous two occasions. It was answered on the fourth ring by the man himself. Introducing himself, Vaughn explained about the discovery of an unusual doll at the scene of a crime. Relating Grace's decades-old memory, and describing the doll found alongside Kemp, he had a sudden doubt — it seemed such a tenuous link. But his fears were unfounded, as Kugelbreck recalled the dolls perfectly well.

'Trust Humphrey to remember something like that,' Kugelbreck chuckled. 'Yes, I have seen a doll just like that. It was quite remarkable. In fact, I made an offer for the whole set, but was turned down.'

'Can you remember any of the other dolls?' Vaughn asked, pulling the Forrester doll towards him.

'I can do better than that. I can send you a picture if that would help.'

'What?' Vaughn exclaimed.

'Yes. I'm afraid I was a little unscrupulous about that. I was at the client's house to appraise some paintings when I saw the dolls. After I'd failed to persuade the owner to sell them to me, I took the opportunity to use my last plate to take a photograph of them as well as the paintings I needed to show to my employer at the time. I still have it somewhere. I'm a keen photographer and I keep all my work.'

'That would be wonderful if you can,' Vaughn said, elated that he might finally be getting somewhere.

'I'm pretty certain I can. You were wondering about the other dolls? I haven't looked at that photograph in years, but I think there were six of them. Yes, I'm pretty sure there were. I know there was the dark-haired one that looked like my uncle Joseph, and a rather fat woman dressed as a cook. Then I think there was a kind of tavern owner with a jolly face and big moustache. I can't remember the rest.'

'Do you happen to remember what colour hair the one with the moustache had?' Vaughn said, looking at the Forrester doll.

'Hmm. I'm not sure, and my photograph wouldn't help, as it's black and white.'

'No matter. Could you possibly see if you can find it for me and then call me back? I can arrange for someone to make a copy for me.'

'It would be my pleasure to help. Has one of them turned up as stolen goods then?' Kugelbreck asked interestedly.

'Not quite, although it may have been stolen at some point,' Vaughn answered cagily. 'My last question is about the owner of these dolls. Do you remember his name?'

'Yes, I wrote it on the back of the photograph as I hoped to make another attempt at buying them. I was never successful, and in 1935 I moved to Amsterdam. When I returned, it was too late.'

'What do you mean?' Vaughn asked, his heart sinking.

'The dolls were owned by one Salomon von Beck, a wealthy Jewish jeweller who lived in a beautiful house on the outskirts of Vienna. He refused point blank to part with the dolls, as they had been made by his great-grandfather. I'm afraid that von Beck and his family disappeared during the war, as did so many others. Even the house was bombed out of existence. It's most fortunate that his dolls seem to have survived.'

I doubt whether Kemp, Forrester and Willoughby would have shared that sentiment, Vaughn thought to himself. That aside, he could not help but let out a groan of disappointment. To come so close to a real clue only to meet a dead end was sickening. If it really was a dead end. 'You say that von Beck and his family disappeared. Do you mean they fled from persecution or they were captured?'

'I'm not sure. I only know for certain that by 1946, when I was able to make some enquiries, there was no sign of them. From the few times I met Salomon, I thought him a very practical man. With his money, he could have left Austria before life became intolerable for Jews. In that case, I believe he would have taken the dolls with him if at all possible. They would have fitted into a reasonably sized trunk. I'm sure that I've never seen or heard of any of them appearing on the market, and they were not the kind of treasure that the Nazis would have been that interested in taking.'

'So von Beck's descendants could still be in possession of the collection, if they survived.'

'And if the doll you have found is Uncle Joseph's doppelgänger, Inspector.' Kugelbreck paused and cleared his throat. 'Would I be permitted to ask exactly how you come to be asking about all this? I'm beginning to wonder if there's more to it than a burglary.'

'It'll probably be in the international newspapers soon enough, I suppose. We've found two dolls matching the descriptions of the 'Uncle Joseph' and 'Tavern Owner' dolls that you saw. There's also a third doll of a smartly suited man in a bowler hat. In each case, they were left beside a murdered man who bore an uncanny resemblance to the dolls, and they had been, well . . . tampered with to look like they had died in the same manner. I'm very much afraid we have a serial killer who has not yet finished.'

'*Mein Gott!*' Kugelbreck exclaimed in shock. 'That's terrible! Who would do such a thing?'

'That's what I'm trying to find out. I'm hoping the dolls we have here are the von Beck ones and that I can somehow find out what happened to them since you last saw them. I really need that photograph of yours, Mr Kugelbreck.'

'Can you stay on the telephone?' Kugelbreck asked, his voice trembling a little.

'Yes.'

'I'll be as quick as I can, Inspector.'

Vaughn heard Kugelbreck call out in German to someone else in the house and he waited as the minutes passed by, thankful that the phone bill was being paid by the Greater Manchester Constabulary. Eventually he heard footsteps approaching the phone.

'I've got it!' Kugelbreck almost shouted into the phone.

'Excellent!'

'How shall I get it to you?'

'Don't worry about that. I'll call you back with the arrangements.'

'You must have it as soon as is humanly possible, Inspector. In addition to the 'Uncle', there's the 'Tavern Owner', a very well dressed man with a bowler hat, a priest, a cook and, I'm very sorry to say, a child.'

★ ★ ★

Seventy-seven-year-old Phyllis Montgomery had never heard of Detective Inspector Gregory Vaughn, nor had she heard of the recent spate of unsolved murders. Living as she did, without any friendly neighbours with whom she could gossip and without a television or a radio, hers was a somewhat sheltered existence. For thirty years, since the untimely demise of her husband, she had sought a form of solace by embracing her Catholicism. To this end, she had become an ardent church-goer, and her devoutness had been noticed and rewarded such that one day a couple of years back she had been asked by the priest of Saint Peter's, her local parish church, if she would like to do certain voluntary chores — the flower-arranging and pamphlet distribution, ensuring that all the kneeling stools were in good order, and all the little 'behind the scenes' things that most church-goers took for granted.

There was a christening to be held this evening, and although Phyllis did not know the family, she knew there was quite a bit of organising to be done beforehand. From what Father Kelly had told her, there was a large turnout expected; and seeing as the other volunteer was away visiting relatives in Brighton, she thought it best to arrive early.

Quietly humming her favourite hymn, 'One More Step Along the World I Go', Phyllis made her way up the gravel path, passing the numerous weathered headstones that lay on either side. The hands of the large clock on the church tower indicated it was nearing half-past four. That left just over two hours before the christening was scheduled to take place. Providing everything went to plan, and

Father Kelly did not turn up drunk as he had once or twice in the past, that left plenty of time to get things in order.

The sky darkened as a cloud scudded across the sun and a chill wind picked up, gusting a heap of leaves into the air. Phyllis stopped and shivered. She would later tell the police that she had felt a sudden inexplicable tingle, an indefinable sense of dread, moments before the church door edged open and Death rushed out.

* * *

'Hell's teeth!' exclaimed Vaughn, shaking his head in disgust. He gazed at the blood-spattered priest's corpse: the dark, sticky crimson blood stood out starkly against the white vestments. The victim lay half-slouched against the altar with one arm draped over it, reaching for the large crucifix that rested atop it as though in search of final absolution. An obscene puddle of blood, in which a footprint had been stamped, caught his eye.

'What kind of sicko murders someone

in a church?' Tyler asked incredulously.

'The worst kind.' Vaughn crouched down in order to get a better look at the blood-drenched corpse, scrutinising it for anything that might be of importance. Hughes had been sent for, but until he arrived to carry out a more detailed investigation, Vaughn had to rely on his own preliminary findings. It was perfectly clear that the priest had been repeatedly stabbed, perhaps up to twenty times. The level of brutality was sickening. It was as though the killer had wanted to make absolutely certain his victim was dead.

At the base of the altar, its cloth body slashed by deep cuts and smeared with blood, was doll number four. Propped beside it was a brown envelope. There was no sign of the murder weapon.

'The priest's name is Father Ernest Kelly,' Tyler revealed. He nodded to a side room at the back of the church. 'The witness is a Mrs Phyllis Montgomery. Needless to say, the poor woman's in one hell of a state. PCs Foster and Kent are with her at the moment. From what I can gather, she saw the killer, and her description matches the one given by Andy Wilkes. I guess it must've given her the fright of her life.'

Vaughn got to his feet. There was a steely resolution in his grey eyes. 'I'm going to get this bastard.' He glanced up at the large wall-mounted crucifix. 'So help me God. If it's the last thing I do, I'm going to get him.' He turned as he heard a commotion at the entrance to the church and was relieved to see Hughes come striding along the aisle.

'Nasty,' Hughes commented on seeing the body. 'Very nasty. Haven't seen one like this for a long time. A frenzied attack. Cause of death, multiple stab wounds.' Removing a cotton bud from a pocket, he knelt down and dipped it into the bloody puddle. 'The level of congealment suggests death occurred little more than an hour ago. Most of the wounds are to the chest and lower abdomen. There are also marks to both arms where he tried to defend himself.'

'Do you think the killer attacked him from the front?' Vaughn asked.

Hughes got to his feet. 'Without a

proper examination I can't be one hundred percent certain, but the nature of the injuries would certainly suggest that.' He noticed the doll. 'So it's another of these, is it?'

'The last of these, if I can help it,' Vaughn said, anger coursing through him. He had never been a particularly religious man, but the violence of Father Kelly's murder, in his own church, affected him. Nowhere was safe from this homicidal maniac.

'Oh, now. This is interesting,' Hughes murmured.

'What is it?'

'I think that some of these wounds were inflicted *after* death. You see the copious amount of blood that flowed out of these wounds. His clothes are soaked. Now, look at these two. The cloth is ripped but only just stained. The heart had stopped pumping by that point. It could mean the killer wasn't sure the man was dead, or perhaps he felt particular animosity towards this victim.'

'He may have been the only one who had a chance to fight back,' Vaughn mused. 'Kemp had no time, Forrester was attacked from behind, and Willoughby literally didn't know what hit him. The priest, on the other hand, saw his attacker and tried to defend himself.'

Hughes sat back on his heels, regarding the corpse with compassion. 'It's a horrible way to die. It also may have been a frightening experience for the killer.'

Vaughn snorted. 'I'll save my sympathy for the innocent!'

* * *

Vaughn's mood was black as he returned to the police station. He could not have prevented Kemp's death, but the other three lay heavily on his conscience. Walking in through the entrance, he heard someone call his name and decided to ignore them. He did not want to talk to anyone just then. The call came again, more insistently, and he turned round with a glare. It was Constable Wilkes, and he had a package in his hands.

'Excuse me, sir, but there's just been a delivery for you, from the Foreign Office!'

Wilkes said excitedly.

Vaughn's attitude changed immediately. 'At last! Thank you,' he said, taking the package and striding with it to his office. He carefully opened it and slid out a protective wallet. Inside were two images: one rather small and another that was an enlargement of it. They showed an ornately decorated glass-fronted cabinet with six dolls standing inside it. His heart beat loudly in his chest. There they all were: Kemp, Forrester, Willoughby and Father Kelly. Not perfect portraits of the dead men, but close enough to be unnerving. The next doll in line was a plump older woman with her hair in a bun and wearing an apron. She was holding a spoon in one hand and a mixing bowl in the other. The final, smaller doll was a boy, possibly in his early teens. It was dressed in a black suit with a hat to match, and Vaughn could just make out the pale, unsmiling face beneath.

The door opened and Wishbourne marched in. 'Let me see it then,' he demanded.

Vaughn moved aside and they both stared at the black-and-white photographs in silence for a few moments.

Wishbourne let out a heavy breath. 'It's them all right, isn't it?'

'There can be no doubt,' Vaughn agreed. 'I mean, look at that one — the Willoughby doll. You can see there's a slight tear on the lapel of his jacket that's been repaired. That's identical to the one we've got.'

'The killer found very good matches for the dolls,' Wishbourne observed, picking up the larger photograph to study it more closely. 'I take it the second doll's moustache is ginger in real life, like Forrester's?'

'Kugelbreck couldn't remember. I think it's actually a bit longer in the photograph. Maybe he trimmed it to match Forrester's style.'

'I want this man caught!' Wishbourne exclaimed. 'Look at what he has planned — the woman and the boy!'

'There are two things we must do immediately,' Vaughn said firmly. He shared the chief superintendent's anger, but they had to keep focused on action, not emotion. 'Firstly, we have to ask for help from the authorities in Austria to track down the von Beck family. We have to know what happened to those dolls after they left Vienna. Secondly, we need to publish this photograph.' He looked challengingly at Wishbourne. He knew that it would feel like the police were admitting failure; but now that they had a clue as to who would be targeted next, they had a duty to warn the public.

Wishbourne did not answer at first. His instinct was to defend his constabulary from its critics, but there was really no choice. 'You're right, Vaughn.' He looked at his watch. 'I'm not sure if we're in time for the morning papers, but we can get a press conference on to tonight's news. It's going to cause panic, but there's no avoiding that. Better to be safe than sorry.' He looked older than usual, the stress of the investigation beginning to get to him. 'What do you think the effect will be on the killer?'

'That's a good question, sir. I'd guess

that he'll be angry and quite possibly scared if he feels everyone is looking out for him.'

'Good!' Wishbourne growled. 'Turn the tables for once.'

'Not necessarily good,' Vaughn disagreed. 'It could make him even more desperate to complete his murders. Yes, it might make him more careless, but it could also make him more dangerous.' He shoved his hands into his pockets to stop the slight nervous shake that had begun to develop. 'To be honest, if I could get the population of Manchester into one place and protect them with armed guards, I would.'

'I know how you feel, but if our guess that the killer is from around here is right, you'd be shutting him in with them.' Wishbourne shook his head and put the photograph down on the table. 'Right. I'll set up the news conference. You get on to Interpol; see if they've any records of criminal activity involving members of this von Beck family. I take it you've already searched our own records?'

'Yes, as soon as I got the name from

Kugelbreck. There wasn't anything on the UK database.'

'Well get one of the lads ringing round the various constabularies asking about the name. It's unusual, and you know as well as I do that there are a lot of people we have suspicions about who never get formally approached. Someone might remember something.'

'Yes, sir. Ideally we want to know where the von Becks and their worldly goods ended up. I've an idea of someone I can ask for advice.'

'Then get on to it.'

★ ★ ★

Despite the failing light, the station was a hive of activity. All those who were not engaged on other cases were roped into the investigation. Tyler was coordinating the systematic phoning of the other police forces. Hughes was performing the largely unnecessary autopsy on Father Kelly in case he had missed anything. Wishbourne was agonising over what to say to the news crew who had eagerly replied to his summons. Vaughn was in his office, talking to a member of the British Embassy in Austria — the same man who had arranged the collection of Kugelbreck's photograph.

'So you see my problem,' Vaughn said as he finished his explanation. 'I must find out what happened to the von Beck family. Did they stay in Vienna? Did they move abroad, perhaps to Britain? Did they even survive the war?'

'It's the most bizarre story I've ever heard!' the official, Robert Lewis, exclaimed. 'I believe you, Inspector. I don't mean to imply otherwise. It's just . . . so crazy. People are actually being killed simply because they look like these dolls?'

'I'm afraid so. Do you think you can help me?'

'Yes, probably. There are fairly good records for finding executed or displaced families. In fact, my family were originally from Austria, further to the west, near Salzburg. They got out in 1935 and came to England. It's one of the reasons I wanted to work out here. I can certainly put some people on to searching the records, and I know most of the local rabbis; they might remember something.'

'With all haste, please. When your family came here, how did they go about it?'

'We were lucky. My grandfather had a cousin in Birmingham, in the jewellery trade. He made the arrangements for us. I'm afraid the experiences of Jews fleeing persecution varied widely. I'll find out what I can for you.'

'Needle in a bloody haystack,' Vaughn said to himself after he had rung off.

Tyler opened the door in time to hear him. 'Yes, but the more people you have looking for the needle, the more likely you are to find it. After the press conference, there'll be thousands on the lookout for the killer.'

'True enough, although I can't help thinking we'll also get a lot of false alarms out of this. Wishbourne has already cancelled all leave so we can have enough people on the ground to respond.'

'If we catch him, I don't see any of us complaining about the work. The whole station wants to get him,' Tyler said. 'Nothing so far from around the country, except all the stations we've talked to want to know the details. The guys up in Glasgow said they're jealous because we've got the best crime going at the moment.'

'Bloody Jocks! They wouldn't be so cavalier about it if they'd seen the bodies,' Vaughn retorted, but he knew that a black sense of humour often went with the job.

'As soon as we get that photograph on TV and in newspapers we'll put a stop to the murders, I'm sure of it.' Tyler was getting caught up in the excitement of a major investigation. 'The killer will have to go to ground, and we can take our time to track him down.'

'You're making a big assumption there,' Vaughn said heavily. The younger man's optimism was beginning to annoy him. 'You're assuming he cares about getting caught. If he's as obsessed as I think he is, that may not matter to him at all.'

7

Mistaken Identity

Since arriving at the station two hours earlier, Vaughn and Tyler had sifted through over a dozen reports from members of the public who believed that they had either seen the killer or were themselves potential victims. Most of these could be quickly discounted, but a few looked promising, and Vaughn had arranged for them to come into the station to be followed up. The press had also set up camp outside, hoping for further revelations.

Taking a short break from the operations room they had set up, Vaughn had taken a coffee through to his office and was examining Kugelbreck's photograph. He had gone over the grainy image with a magnifying glass, picking out the fine details of each face; scrutinising each in the hope that somehow it would provide him with the breakthrough he so desperately sought. The more he stared at the dolls, the more they seemed to play on his mind; and knowing that four people had met dreadful deaths as a result of them was having an effect on him that was most unwelcome. He had no time whatsoever for the supernatural, believing only in that which he could see, hear and touch; but nonetheless he found himself entertaining the idea that the dolls *were* cursed. Certainly they had brought nothing but death to those who had the misfortune of bearing a similar likeness.

For some reason, he found himself continually drawn to the doll on the far right — that of the boy dressed in funereal attire. As he had told Roza Weizak, he had never liked dolls, and there was something genuinely creepy and unsettling about this one. He gulped nervously as he gazed into the doll's dead eyes, and for a moment he could have sworn it had given a knowing wink.

In a sudden dark flash of memory, he saw himself as a young boy, standing on the bank of a neglected canal. In his hands was his sister's doll, which he had come to hate and fear. Like an unwanted newborn, it seemed to be wriggling in his grasp, kicking and screaming at him, yelling at him not to do it. Unmercifully, he cast it far into the sluggish, dirty water. It submerged, then surfaced, and for one terrible moment he imagined it swimming towards him . . .

Vaughn jerked in his chair, aware that his imagination was getting the better of him. He jumped as there was a loud knock on his office door.

The door opened and Tyler entered. Behind him was a large frumpy woman in a grey raincoat, her hair up in thick curlers under a headscarf. Behind her was a thin-faced, bespectacled man. There was an impoverished look to them both and, somewhat judgementally, Vaughn reasoned that they were probably not the most educated pair to ever enter his office.

'Sir, this is Jim and Sally Jenkins.' Tyler ushered the strangers inside before making a hurried exit.

'Good morning.' Rising from his chair, Vaughn stopped suddenly and shuddered. The woman — Mrs Jenkins — was the living embodiment of the female doll. Admittedly she was not dressed as a cook, and her hair was different, but . . . the face. Chubby, hamster-cheeked, double-chinned. Apart from the cigarette hanging from her trembling lips, the similarities were staggering.

'I'm Sally Jenkins. I saw the news last night and, well, here I am.' Noticing the enlarged photograph on the desk, Sally pointed at it, singling out 'her' doll. She took a nervous puff of her cigarette. 'I've no idea how that was done . . . but that's just like me, isn't it? I knew as soon as I saw it. I said to you, didn't I, Jim, how uncanny it was that — '

'If my wife's in danger I want you to do something!' interrupted Jenkins. With a scarred and tattooed hand, he straightened his ill-fitting false teeth. 'I don't pay my taxes so that you lot can sit about here drinking coffee.' He pointed an accusatory finger at Vaughn's cup. 'You need to get this bastard and bang him up.'

'Please, calm down.' Despite the awkwardness of the situation, Vaughn was relieved that here was one potential victim they had managed to get to before the killer. Now, if they could just get her to sit in a cell under twenty-four police protection . . . Or use her as bait, some dark thought suggested.

'Calm down? How the hell do you expect me to calm down?' Sally protested. She slumped into a chair and began to cry. 'I'm going to be murdered.'

'Nonsense,' Vaughn said in what he hoped was a soothing voice. 'You've done the right thing by coming here, Mrs Jenkins. You're perfectly safe. Please stop crying. Nothing's going to happen to you. Now, what we're going to do is ensure that — ' He was interrupted by Tyler's reappearance.

'Sir, I . . . I'm afraid there's been another one.'

Vaughn's heart lurched. The fact that Sally Jenkins was here could only mean one thing — the killer had got to the child. Taking a deep breath, he closed his eyes for a moment, then reopened them.

He felt sick to the core. 'Where?' he mumbled.

'St. John's; the high school off Cromwell Street.

Vaughn cursed volubly.

Through tear-filled eyes, Sally looked up. 'Did you say St. John's?'

Tyler nodded.

'But . . . but that's where Moira works.' Sally brought a trembling hand to her mouth and turned to look at her husband.

'Moira?' Vaughn asked.

'She's Sally's sister,' said Jenkins. 'Her identical twin. She's a dinner lady there.'

★ ★ ★

'Moira Stillwell was found dead this morning by another one of the dinner ladies,' announced Lockwood as he guided Vaughn and Tyler along the empty school corridors towards the kitchen. He held open a door permitting the two policemen to enter.

At first Vaughn could see nothing out of place. It looked just as he expected a school kitchen to look. There were sinks, tables for preparing the food, shelves filled with stacked plates and utensils. To his right he saw the large serving hatch, and to his left . . . He stopped. The tiled floor was a mess, littered with smashed crockery and unopened tins of custard.

'She's in here,' said Lockwood, opening a side door. 'I haven't touched anything yet. In fact, I only got here a short time ago myself. Hughes wanted to finish up on the cadaver we were examining.'

The room Vaughn entered was a small storeroom. Opposite him, he could see a large chest freezer. Lockwood opened it and stepped aside.

Vaughn advanced. He grimaced upon seeing the frozen carcass: the fat, rock-solid face, mouth open as though it was shouting in agony, was encased in a white powdering of frost. The eyes were wide and staring and had a terrible look to them. The exposed skin was blue and puffy.

At the end of the freezer, close to the victim's feet, amidst the bags of frozen peas and carrots and the boxes of ready-to-defrost burgers, pies and sausages, was the doll. In the poor light it looked like a small snowman; and had it not been for the brown envelope which lay nearby, it could easily have been mistaken for one. Red claw marks ran down the inside of the freezer lid.

'She was still alive when she was put inside?' Vaughn said, speaking more to himself than anyone else.

Lockwood nodded in agreement. 'I'm afraid so. Acute hypothermia would have set in during the first twenty minutes or so, and the core body temperature would have plummeted sharply. In addition, there's no air supply. It would have been a dreadful, protracted way to die, buried alive in a sub-zero coffin. From first sight, there are no visible external injuries on the body, but from the wreckage in the kitchen it's pretty safe to assume that a violent struggle took place there. The killer overpowered the victim and forced her inside.'

Examining the lock, Vaughn saw it had been forced. 'Is there no key?' he asked.

'Apparently not; or rather, it's missing.'

'How long has she . . . ?' Reminded of photographs he had seen of frozen mammoths dug from the Siberian tundra, Vaughn found himself unable to finish the question.

'Hard to say without a full autopsy, but several hours at least. I'd guess that she's been in here overnight and that the attack took place sometime yesterday, possibly in the evening.'

'Before the news bulletin went out, in other words,' commented Tyler.

'From what the headmaster told me, she lived on her own, so that would explain why her failure to return home went unreported. Apparently she was also known to work late, making puddings for the next day.'

'Okay. Tyler, we'll need to interview everyone who was here yesterday evening; see if they saw or heard anything out of the ordinary. I'll speak to the headmaster. Lockwood, do the usual — photographs, fingerprints, anything you can find. Then you can get the body back to Hughes.' Vaughn paused in his list of orders as a thought struck him. 'You'll have to wait for the body to thaw out before the autopsy can be done, won't you?'

'At least it's pretty obvious how the poor woman died,' Tyler said, his voice low. The excitement he had felt yesterday had turned to dismay when they had heard of the latest killing. 'God! How can anyone do that?'

Vaughn regarded the frozen corpse with compassion and anger. He forced himself to remain outwardly calm, but inside he was seething. Another victim he had failed to save. Wishbourne was going to be furious, the press were going to be up in arms, and as for the deceased's twin sister ... Sally Jenkins had been distraught when he had left her at the station. God only knew how she was going to react when they got back with the bad news.

* * *

The operations room was packed. Wishbourne, Vaughn, Tyler and Hughes had been joined by the criminal psychologist, Coleman, and they were allocating sections of the city to the large group of policemen and women who had been assigned to the investigation.

'This is perhaps the worst case we've ever known in the county, and one of the worst in the whole of Britain,' Vaughn addressed the crowd. 'There's very little we can assume about the killer except that he will try to complete the set of doll murders. There's no sane reason for his actions. The patrols covering the local schools are already in place and will be relieved regularly. I want house-to-house enquiries throughout Manchester, concentrating on the areas where the victims lived and worked. Look for signs that a man has been hanging around. He's spotting his victims somewhere and finding out their habits.'

Wishbourne stepped forward. 'I shouldn't need to tell you that there's a real sense of panic out there and the press are tearing us to pieces. But all that doesn't matter. What does is the life of a child. Our primary job is to protect the public, and we're failing dismally.' He pointed to the pictures that had been pinned to the wall.

Five photographs taken of the victims after their deaths were paired with the five dolls that had been recovered: Kemp with his head almost hanging off, Forrester's bloated body in the tank, Willoughby impaled, Father Kelly dead by his altar, and Moira Stillwell the worst image of all. No one who saw her could fail to imagine what it would have been like to die that way.

The final image was just of the child doll. 'It's up to us to make sure that there's never a corpse to match this!' Vaughn concluded firmly.

After all the arrangements had been made and many questions asked and answered, Vaughn and Tyler retired to the former's office. On the desk they found the artist's impression of the killer, taken from Phyllis Montgomery's description of the figure she had seen fleeing from the church.

'Get copies of this out to all the teams,' Vaughn told his detective sergeant.

'That white face . . . do you think he was wearing a mask?' Tyler asked, looking at the sketchy picture. 'Mrs Montgomery said he was as white as a sheet, and so did Andy Wilkes.'

'It's quite possible. This is all tied up with how people look, so there may well be some significance in the killer adopting a disguise. We won't know for sure unless we catch him. We should talk to all the families again. There might be something they haven't realised was important. Meet me back here in ten minutes and we'll start with Kemp's home and office, talk to the neighbours.'

'Yes, sir.' Tyler took the picture from the table and left.

Vaughn lit a cigarette, leant back in his chair and took a much-needed drag.

Five dreadful deaths. Five, as yet, unsolved murders.

Of all the murder investigations Vaughn had worked on in the past, this was by far the most high-profile, and it was proving to have the most profound effect on him. This was probably due to its very strangeness. For the unfortunates who had been murdered were not victims of any normal crime for normal motives. Rather, they were almost like sacrificial victims; innocent members of the public — with the exception of Forrester — who had fallen foul of the warped machinations of a deranged killer with the most unholy of agendas. Vaughn found himself imagining a scenario in which he was interrogating the killer; extracting the answers to the questions he so badly needed. He had little psychological expertise, but over the course of his career he had developed a rudimentary knowledge of the human mind, and he wanted to discover just what motivated such an individual. To consign the killer's action and behaviour to mere madness was too easy. There had to be more to this. Much more.

Tyler returned and they set off for the office Kemp had worked in. On the drive there, they saw two pairs of patrolling squad cars and, passing a school, were pleased to see a very visible police presence.

The office building was above a bookshop and the door to it opened onto a fairly busy shopping area. It would have been easy for the killer to loiter outside, waiting for Kemp to appear in order to follow him home. The manager of the office was happy to help them and gathered his staff to be addressed by Vaughn. When he asked about any strangers, however, they all looked blank. Then the youngest of the secretaries put her hand up. Guessing that she had only recently left school, Vaughn encouraged her to speak.

'There was one thing, but I thought it was something unrelated,' she began, and then stopped.

'Yes? Anything might be important.'

'About a week ago, when I left work, there was a man looking at shoes in the window of the shop opposite. I caught his eye in the reflection and he was staring right at me. I looked away — well you do, don't you? But when I looked back a moment later, he was still staring. I just thought he was a bit of a letch, but maybe he wasn't really looking at me, just at the doorway.'

Vaughn regarded her thoughtfully. She was pretty and looked ill at ease in her smart suit. A girl just getting used to adulthood. It could quite easily have been a man giving her the once-over, but then again maybe not. 'Tell me what he looked like, if you can remember.'

'Old. I mean about my dad's age, thirty-seven or so. He had dark hair and was kind of ordinary. He had a long mackintosh.'

'You mean like a flasher mac?' Vaughn said.

She blushed and nodded. 'I didn't see him there again.'

'Might you recognise him?' Vaughn asked.

'Maybe. I couldn't swear to it, though,' the girl answered cautiously.

'Did anyone else see someone like that?' Vaughn asked the others. There were shakes of the head all round. 'Okay. If you do happen to see him again, call the station and try to get a good look at him. It's probably nothing, but you never know.'

* * *

Next was the place where Willoughby had worked. They had no luck at the barrister's office, but a trip to his three-storey town house was more fruitful. Vaughn had seen Mrs Willoughby before, and his last visit had produced floods of tears. He had formed the impression that she was already emotionally frail, an English Rose who had been loved and protected by her husband. Without his support, she was lost. The charlady who opened the door to the house gave him a hard glare and positioned herself in the doorway.

'Still not caught him, have you? It's all over the papers,' the woman said sourly. 'Poor Mrs Willoughby's beside herself with grief. She's hardly eaten a thing since the murder, so don't you go upsetting her again.'

'*You* may be able to help me, actually,' Vaughn said pleasantly. 'You help out with the household tasks, don't you?'

'I do *all* of them, except for dusting the ornaments. Mrs Willoughby likes doing that. She cooks too, very nicely, although I've been making her sandwiches recently. She just hasn't the appetite anymore.'

'I'm truly sorry for the awful time she's

having. This killer is destroying lives all over the city. What I wondered is if either of you ever noticed someone lingering in the area, someone who could have been following Mr Willoughby.'

'We've been over all that! When I'm here, I'm working too hard to stand and gawp!' the charlady answered indignantly. 'And I'm busy right now.' She thumped her mop down on the front step and folded her arms.

'I appreciate that. When I called on Mrs Willoughby before, I noticed how beautifully kept the house was.' Vaughn felt he was fighting a losing battle but was determined to try. 'I only thought that, as you're clearly very protective of Mrs Willoughby, who struck me as a very gentle person, you'd have been the one to see off unwanted tradesmen and the like.'

'Well, yes. If I'm here I answer the door and there are a few spivs who try to sell us rubbish. I get rid of them sharpish, and I don't recall anyone recently.'

'It's a lovely square,' Vaughn said, looking around the green and well-kept central garden. 'I bet you get people sitting on the benches at lunchtimes.'

'Often. Especially in the nice weather we've had,' the woman answered. Suddenly the colour drained from her face. She turned her head to look at a bench at the other end of the square. 'There . . . there *was* someone. An artist. I'd forgotten all about him.'

'An artist?' Tyler echoed in surprise.

'He had some paper, a sketchpad kind of thing. He was there for a few days, about three weeks ago.'

'Did you ever see if he was really drawing?' Vaughn asked intently.

'Yes, I walked behind him one time, on my way to the shops to pick up some tea. He was a real artist, I mean it was good.'

'And what was he drawing?'

'This house,' the charlady said, her eyes widening as she remembered. 'And he had put in Mr Willoughby too, going out in the morning, with his bowler hat and his briefcase.' She staggered suddenly, her knees buckling. Tyler caught her and lowered her to the steps beside her mop and bucket. 'Do you think it was him?' the woman asked, her strident voice reduced to a croak.

'Can you describe him?' Vaughn asked, his hopes rising.

'Reasonably attractive. Dark hair, under a hat. Not fat, not short. A bit of a tan, I think.'

'And what kind of age?'

'Youngish, I'd guess. Maybe thirties. Oh, God. What if it *was* him?'

'It might have been someone else entirely,' Vaughn said, hoping to calm her down; but excitement was building in him, and the glance he exchanged with Tyler was loaded. The guise of an artist would be a very useful way to keep an eye on someone. 'Just in case though, I'm going to leave Detective Sergeant Tyler here with you to take a full statement, and I'd like to send our own artist round to see if we can get a reasonable photo-fit.'

The woman nodded tearfully. 'I'll do my best.'

Vaughn addressed Tyler. 'I'll send over a WPC too. We'll have to ask Mrs Willoughby if she noticed this man as well, and she's already in a delicate state. Radio in when you've finished here and we'll meet up. I'm going to talk to Mrs Forrester. We might be seeing a pattern here. And when you've got the photo-fit, we can show it to the girl at Kemp's office. See if she recognises it.'

'Very good, sir.'

Vaughn strode back to the car and started the engine. Turning out of the affluent district where Mrs Willoughby lived, he was heading for Forrester's house when the radio crackled into life. He answered it, one hand on the wheel. 'Yes, what is it?'

'DI Vaughn?'

'Yes.'

'This is Constable Harley, sir. Chief Superintendent Wishbourne would like you to come to the station. He has some news.'

'Not another murder!'

'No, sir. I don't think it's anything like that.'

'Okay, I'll be as quick as I can. The traffic's still heavy. Oh, and send a WPC and John Rider to thirty-three Park Square. I need him to draw a potential suspect.' Vaughn put the radio back down and swung the car round at the next junction. His mind was racing. Had one of the many teams found a clue, maybe even caught the killer? Could it be the end of this increasingly nightmarish case?

Eventually he pulled into the police station's car park and bounded up the steps, dashing past the small group of reporters without comment. The chief superintendent and Hughes were waiting for him.

'Come on,' Wishbourne said, leading the way to the operations room. 'There have been a couple of developments.' Once inside, he sat down. 'Hughes found blood under Moira Stillwell's fingernails.'

'Human blood,' Hughes clarified. 'And it's not her own type. She was type A, and this is type B.'

'So she scratched him in the struggle,' Vaughn said.

Hughes nodded. 'Hard enough to draw blood.'

'B. That's not a rare blood type, is it?'

'Sadly not. A and B occur with about the same frequency. But if we do get a suspect and he's not B, we can at least rule him out.'

'And if we find someone with type B who has scratches, they've got some questions to answer. Good work!'

'There's more to come, Vaughn,' Wishbourne said. 'Your Foreign Office contact called for you. He wants you to talk to him. He was still waiting for some more information to come in, but he says that Salomon von Beck definitely died in a concentration camp in 1940. However, his wife, son and daughter-in-law escaped. According to an old rabbi Lewis approached, they were intending to head for England.'

8

A Message Arrives

It had been a long time since such a heavy police presence on the streets of Manchester had been required — not even during the Manchester Derby, when the two home football teams played each other and old scores were settled off the pitch more often than on. Wishbourne had brought in every uniformed officer that could be spared and had accepted offers of help from the surrounding constabularies as well. Even so, many schools had taken the decision to shut down, prompted mostly by the fact that vast numbers of parents had refused to take their children — even the girls — to school until the killer was caught.

While their colleagues were out on patrol, Vaughn and Tyler were following the trail of the von Becks from Vienna to England. The records relating to those seeking asylum were fairly good, but it took time to search through them. They already knew that there were no von Becks listed as resident in Manchester and the surrounding area, but there were a few listings for Beck — Vaughn reasoned that the family might have dropped the highly Germanic *von* — and they were checking through them but were only finding law-abiding citizens so far.

Vaughn had tried calling Robert Lewis as soon as he heard the news from Vienna, but the official had been tied up. Undeterred, he called every hour until he got through.

'Inspector Vaughn! I'm glad you called,' Lewis greeted him.

'I wanted to thank you for the information you sent us. Interpol's come up with nothing,' Vaughn said.

'That's fine. More than happy to help. I can confirm that the remaining von Becks did indeed leave Vienna, and there are records of them entering France in 1938 with the intention of crossing to England and taking up residence in London. It looks like Salomon stayed behind to wind up his business affairs, but he left it too late. Now, I'm not sure if you're aware that a large number of Jewish migrants altered their names to fit into their new countries. My own family was Levy until my father changed it to Lewis.'

'Well, I've been searching for anyone called Beck, and we've found a few but they seem to be blameless,' Vaughn informed him. 'We can't find any record of an official name change from von Beck for anyone that matches the ages of the three adults, but I guess a lot of that was done informally. After all, if you arrive saying your papers got destroyed in the bombing, there would have been no easy way of checking.'

'That's right. You should also try any names that may have been derived from the original meaning,' Lewis urged. 'Beck means a stream or brook. That might give you a lead. Although a fair number of people choosing a new name simply picked anything that struck them as being British. Even the royal family became Windsor instead of Saxe Coburg-Gotha during the First World War. If your killer is a descendent of Salomon von Beck, he might now be called John Smith.'

'Well, there's a cheery thought,' Vaughn muttered.

'Have you contacted the local synagogues?' Lewis continued. 'They might know if any of their congregation came from Vienna, maybe even know their original name.'

'I'll get on to that,' Vaughn said, silently cursing himself for not having thought of it before.

'Of course, there's no guarantee that your man is an observant Jew, but his parents might be if they're still alive. I think we have to assume that Salomon's wife, Miriam, will be dead by now, as she'd be well into her nineties.'

'I'll get straight on to it.'

'And you still don't know if the killer actually is a member of the family?' Lewis commented.

'In the absence of other evidence, we have to follow every possible lead.' Vaughn found he was gritting his teeth. Lewis was merely voicing his own doubts, but it was still galling to hear.

'Well, good luck, Inspector. If I hear anything more, I'll call you.'

With an angry puff of breath, Vaughn replaced the handset and waited impatiently while Tyler finished the call he was engaged on. Then he said to him: 'We need a list of all the synagogues in Manchester, and start looking for any names that are similar to 'stream' or 'brook'. Hughes is the crossword fan. I'll get the thesaurus from his office to check for other synonyms.' He strode off, leaving Tyler scrabbling for the phonebook.

The station corridors were strangely quiet, almost eerie, with most out looking for the killer or protecting the schools. Vaughn walked quickly to the pathologist's room and pulled the book from its customary place. Flicking through the pages, he found the right entry and began to read as he walked back. Halfway there, he slowed and then stopped. One of the synonyms had almost jumped off the page at him. The list read: stream, rivulet, creek and burn. An image of Cyril Burns came to his mind — an ordinary-looking man in his thirties, with dark hair and slightly olive skin that could be mistaken for a tan.

Tyler looked up in surprise as his immediate superior skidded into the operations room. 'Grab your coat! I want you to bring in Cyril Burns immediately!' Vaughn shouted. 'Take PCs Wilkes and Hansby with you.'

'Cyril Burns?' Tyler was confused.

'Burns. It's Scottish for brook. It might be him.'

Tyler's eyes widened and he snatched up his coat. 'The photo-fit *could* be him I suppose, but I'd have thought him a bit too normal to be the right man.'

'It's too much of a coincidence not to check it out,' Vaughn retorted. 'Or do you want to explain to grieving parents why we didn't follow up every possibility?'

Less than a minute later, a car sped out of the station.

★   ★   ★

Cyril Burns was marched into Vaughn's office. He looked very different from the man they had met at the factory. Gone were the working man's non-descript clothes. Instead, Burns wore a colourful patchwork waistcoat over a pair of jeans. He also smelled faintly of pot.

Vaughn raised an eyebrow at Tyler, who nodded. 'We found evidence of drug use at Mr Burns's flat, and he appears to be under the influence of a controlled substance,' Tyler said, forcing the surprised and indignant hippie into a chair.

'You can't just drag me out of my home! I'll have a lawyer on to you. I know my rights!'

'If we find evidence that you're dealing drugs, then we have every right to bring you in,' Vaughn said evenly. Inside, he was torn between satisfaction at unsettling the arrogant agitator, and worry that he looked even less a likely fit for the murderer. There was no reason not to grill him anyway, so he started. 'You can of course refuse to speak without a lawyer present, but I'd like you to hear what my questions are first of all.'

'I'm saying nothing,' Burns said stubbornly, then immediately contradicted himself. 'It's tough work, you know, being a spy. I need to wind down a bit sometimes.'

'I'm interested in your family history,' Vaughn continued as if there had been no interruption.

'What?'

'Who are your parents? Where did they grow up? That kind of thing. If you feel you need a lawyer present, then by all means you can wait in a cell until one arrives.'

'This is ridiculous!'

'Are you refusing to answer?' Vaughn asked.

'No. But I don't see the point of this.' Burns did not know what to make of the situation. He looked from Tyler to Vaughn as if searching for some clue, then finally started to talk. 'Okay, my father is a Mancunian, through and through. Son and grandson of honest working Salford men. His name's Gerald. My mother, Iphigenia, is Greek. She and her family arrived here in the 1950s and started up a restaurant. It's along Castle Street. I used to help out there when I was a teenager.

You can check it out.'

Vaughn had been looking at Burns's bare arms while the man spoke. There was no trace of any scratches there, or on his face. This was looking increasingly like a dead end. He stood up and signalled Tyler to join him in the corridor.

'I really don't think it's him, sir,' Tyler said. 'His flat's like something out of a film — Indian stuff everywhere, and several interesting plants we should take a closer look at, but nothing relating to the doll murders.'

'Maybe, but I want you to check the records for his parents. Get their full names and dates of birth. I think you're right, but I'm not releasing him until I'm sure. If he starts crying for a lawyer, get him one, but don't hurry over it. Oh, and get a blood sample from him.' Vaughn ran his fingers through his thick grey hair. 'I had a moment there where it seemed so obvious. I'll be in the operations room if you need me.'

He walked down the corridor, heading for the pack of cigarettes in his office. He was almost there when he heard a crashing sound a little way off and then raised voices. Turning round, he followed the voices to one of the rooms at the back of the station. There were two policemen staring in astonishment at an object on the ground. They turned round to him, looking equally surprised to see him.

'There's . . . there's been a delivery for you, sir,' one of the constables said, a hint of a nervous laugh in his voice.

'What do you mean?' Vaughn asked irritably, striding over to them. There on the carpet was an old brick, and tied around it was a piece of paper. It was addressed to him.

'We were having our break and this just came hurtling through the window.'

'Did you see who threw it?'

'No. By the time we got to the window there was no one around.'

'Okay. Let's see what we've got here.' Vaughn picked up the paper-wrapped brick and undid the string. There was a note in the same handwriting as the doll letters:

Detective Inspector Vaughn

It has come to my attention that you are investigating a series of 'murders'. I must demand that you cease this instantly. You no doubt have the best of intentions, but you do not comprehend the nature of my actions. The bodies you have mistaken for people are just the outer manifestations of an evil that has afflicted my family for many years.

I believe you to be a good man, and I bear you no ill will, but I warn you that if you do not end your interference I will have to stop you. My life is at stake.

Now that I know the secret to their destruction, I must not be impeded and will kill any who stand in my way.

Vaughn grinned, a strangely wolfish expression on his face. 'We've got him rattled,' he said to the constables who had been waiting expectantly as he read the letter. He pointed to the taller man. 'It's Atkins, isn't it?'

'Yes, sir.'

'Go get Dr Hughes. Tell him that I need him in the operations room. Wishbourne too.' Vaughn turned to the other man. 'You — er . . . '

'Redcliffe, sir,' the other supplied.

'Okay, Redcliffe. Go outside and see if there's any trace of our brick-slinger or anyone who saw him do it. I think there's a bus stop along that road, so we may be lucky. Oh, and let Detective Sergeant Tyler know there's been a development and he's to come and find me as soon as he can get away.'

★ ★ ★

'You mean to tell me that someone saw a nutter throw a brick through our window and wasn't going to report it?' Wishbourne was incensed.

'The woman in question is quite old, and she might have missed her bus,' Redcliffe replied apologetically. 'I was only just able to get her details before it arrived.'

'No sense of civic duty,' Wishbourne complained.

'Well, sir. The light is fading. She does have poor eyesight, so she can't give us a description, and she said she thought we'd probably noticed the attack. She was expecting to see coppers leaping out of the window in pursuit.'

'And so she should have! The two of you were useless.'

'To be fair, Chief Superintendent,' Vaughn stepped in, 'there's an alleyway out there that meant he could be out of sight almost immediately.'

'Why are you looking so damned perky, Vaughn?'

'Because we're getting to him,' Vaughn said. 'I think he was ready to strike and we stopped him. There's another reason too. I've just come from the front desk. A family have come in to ask for police protection for their son. I've met him and he's the spitting image of the final doll. His name's Brian Garwood; attends a school that's now heavily protected. It's one of the first ones we got uniforms out to and it probably saved his life. I've put the family in the canteen with two officers for now.'

'Oh, well, that's good news.' Wishbourne struggled to bring his emotions back under control.

'The canteen's only windows overlook an internal courtyard,' Vaughn said. 'It's completely safe.'

'Yes, good choice, Inspector.'

Hughes cleared his throat. 'The handwriting looks identical to me except for being a little more irregular. I think that's due to stress. I'm happy to swear to it being from the same person who penned the doll letters.'

'Any fingerprints?' Vaughn asked hopefully.

'No, but paper's not very good for that, I'm afraid,' Hughes said, shaking his head. 'Neither's brick, for that matter.'

'Okay. The question now is — 'Vaughn broke off, hearing shouting nearby. 'It's a bit early for the drunks,' he observed, noting that it was only seven o'clock on a weekday, and opened the door to the corridor.

The sounds were much clearer now, and he deduced there was an angry argument at the front desk. It was a fairly common occurrence, and he made to close the door when he heard a familiar name. Someone, a man, was demanding to see Cyril Burns. Vaughn went to investigate, listening as he did so.

'I know you've nicked the bastard. I want a go at him; I've got a right to!'

Turning the corner of the corridor, Vaughn saw what was happening. Joe Forrester was being restrained by two constables and was yelling the place down.

'Hello again, Mr Forrester,' Vaughn greeted him calmly.

'You!' Forrester exclaimed. 'You've got Burns in here, and I demand to see the bastard that killed my dad.'

'Exactly how did you know that Cyril Burns is here?'

'Someone saw him being carted off, someone who cares!' Forrester spat back.

'It's a shame that someone hasn't got their facts straight,' Vaughn said, folding his arms. 'Mr Burns is not suspected of being involved in any deaths.'

'No, *you've* got it wrong.' Forrester spat on the floor. 'Gerry Nielson's been keeping an eye on Burns since the toerag quit the factory. He told me what Burns looked like, and I remembered a bloke like that was hanging around my pub a few weeks ago. He was stalking Dad!'

Vaughn felt the hair on the back of his neck stand up. 'Hang on a minute. You say there was a man matching Burns's description at your pub?'

'That's what I said. Are you stupid?' Forrester sneered. 'You've got the killer there and you don't even know it.'

Vaughn moved closer to Forrester, so close he could smell his malodorous breath. 'Cyril Burns is not the man. A simple blood test proved that. However, if you're right about there being a similar man following your father, I want to know everything you can tell me.' He gazed coldly at Forrester. 'If you'd had the decency to cooperate with us earlier, it might have prevented the other murders.' He motioned to the two constables who were still holding on to Forrester's arms. 'Escort him to an interview room and ask Detective Sergeant Tyler to bring along the photo-fit.'

'I want a lawyer!' Forrester immediately barked out.

'Why? Have you got something to hide?' Vaughn shot back.

'No. I just . . . ' Forrester faltered. The anger that had propelled him to the police station was being replaced by uncertainty.

'Good,' Vaughn said with a tone of finality. He led them down towards the interview rooms and felt a sudden rush of adrenaline as he saw Tyler and Burns coming towards them. The detective sergeant was obviously moving the man to a cell to await his lawyer. Tensed for trouble, Vaughn kept a steady pace and raised his hand in greeting to Tyler. 'Can I have a word?' he said lightly.

The two parties paused, and Forrester looked uninterestedly at Burns and the accompanying constable. There was not the barest flicker of recognition between the two men. Tyler had looked momentarily surprised, but had the intelligence to follow the inspector's lead and answered a few unimportant questions.

A few minutes later he joined them in the small and claustrophobic interview room, bringing the photo-fit that Willoughby's charlady had helped to create. 'So, Mr Forrester, can you tell me what the suspicious individual looked like?'

'Jet-black hair, dirty-looking skin,' Forrester said. 'Weird, staring eyes.'

'So, Mediterranean, would you say? What age?'

'Between thirty and forty, maybe. I'm not good at guessing.'

'Do you think you'd recognise him again?' Vaughn asked.

'Certain of it. I don't like having foreign types in my pub. You can't trust 'em. Vince Cooper would be sure to recognise him too. He props up the bar most nights and he talks to everybody whether they want him to or not.' Forrester's limited patience was running out once more. 'Look, are you sure Burns didn't do it?'

'Positive. You walked past him not five minutes ago and didn't so much as bat an eyelid.' Vaughn watched the shock register.

'You mean that hippy freak? That's Burns?' Forrester asked in disbelief.

'Yes.'

'Oh. Well, I've never seen him before in my life,' Forrester admitted.

'What about this man?' Vaughn opened the envelope containing the photo-fit and slid the picture to Forrester.

The reaction was immediate. Forrester leapt up from his chair, knocking it over. 'That's him!'

* * *

The drive to The Crown had given Vaughn and Tyler time to talk and exchange information. Both Burns and Forrester would be kept at the station for a while — Burns to be questioned about drugs and Forrester ostensibly to make a full statement, but mostly to keep him out of the way. He had said that the 'permanent resident' Vince Cooper would be sure to be at the bar, and they wanted to get his opinion. The barmaid pointed out an old man sitting at the end of the bar nursing a half-pint of bitter.

Vaughn introduced himself and bought Cooper another drink. 'I understand you know all of the regulars here?' he said.

'Each and every one. They're like my family,' Cooper claimed, slightly drunkenly.

'What about the men who just visit a few times? Are you good at remembering faces?'

'You won't find a better memory than mine, Inspector.'

'Then can you tell me if this man looks familiar?' Vaughn produced the photo-fit that had so electrified Forrester.

'Oh, yes. I know him,' Cooper said measuredly. 'He hasn't been in for a bit though. He never had much of a thirst on him, not like me.' He looked hopefully at his diminishing pint.

'Do you know his name?' Vaughn continued, ignoring the hint.

'That's Michael Brooks,' Cooper answered.

Vaughn and Tyler looked at each other in excitement. Tyler flicked open his notebook.

'What can you tell us about him?' Vaughn asked. He was working hard to keep his elation from showing.

'Not much. He doesn't like to talk. I

got him going once though. I'd just been to a funeral and was talking about it to Lisa here.' The old drinker indicated the barmaid. 'Brooks suddenly said he'd worked for an undertaker for a while. He said he had to give it up because his granny didn't approve.'

'His granny?'

'Yes, I thought it was funny too!' Cooper laughed, misinterpreting Vaughn's tone. 'A grown man chucking a good honest job in cause his old granny took offence.'

'Wasn't it something religious, Vince?' the barmaid chimed in.

'That's right. I think she was a Yid, and they do things differently.'

'Do you happen to know where he lives?' Vaughn asked urgently. All the pieces were falling into place at long last.

'As it happens, I do.' Vince tapped his empty glass and Vaughn instantly called for a refill. 'One time I was coming back from my daughter's house and I saw Michael turning down Ackerman's Lane. I was going to follow him and tease him about that granny of his. He went into one of those rundown places near the canal. It was number nineteen, like my bus. It surprised me. I thought they were all up for demolition.'

'Are you sure he actually went into the house?'

'Yes. He had a key and he went in. He must live there, or why else would he have a key?'

'Why else indeed?' Vaughn allowed himself a moment to savour the feeling of elation. He slapped a five-pound note on the counter. 'Have a few more on me, Vince.' So saying, he patted the old man between the shoulders and led Tyler out.

'Bloody hell! Do you think this is it?' Tyler asked the moment they were back in the car and heading for the station.

'It's all coming together. I want to do some checks on this Michael Brooks, but it feels like we're on to something. What we can't do is go rushing off there. Wishbourne will need to get us a search warrant, and I want to find out if there's any record of Brooks at that address, or his grandmother. Now we have a name, we can really ferret around.'

'Sir, I don't want to criticise, but can

you drive a bit slower?' Tyler said, hanging on to the seat.

'No. There's too much to do,' Vaughn replied firmly, and sped on.

★ ★ ★

'I've found them!' The cry had gone up from a constable in the operations room. He had been searching through the 1971 census records.

'Brilliant! What have you got?' Vaughn asked, hurrying over to the table.

'Miriam Brooks, widow, ninety-one; and Michael Brooks, undertaker's assistant, thirty. Living at nineteen Ackerman's Lane.'

'So they changed from von Beck to Brooks. I wonder what happened to Michael's parents. And he must have been born in Britain. Start searching the records for births that might be him. I want to know everything possible.'

Tyler came into the room, followed by Wishbourne. 'I've got a team together for the raid, sir. They're all ready to go.'

'And the search warrant is taken care

of,' Wishbourne said.

Vaughn checked the time. It was several minutes past two o'clock in the morning. They had decided to mount a dawn raid. With the sixth target, Brian Garwood, safely asleep at the station, it was felt they could afford the time to do it properly rather than take their chances against an armed and extremely dangerous man. It was always better to catch a suspect unawares, and a squad of policemen breaking the door down in the early hours of the morning had yielded good results in the past.

'Okay, we'll move off shortly.' Vaughn looked once more at the photographs of the five victims to strengthen his resolve. Then he addressed the room. 'Those of you who are staying here. Firstly, thank you for the work you've all put in. Secondly, keep at it! If we arrest Brooks, I want a watertight case to bring against him. Just imagine how you'd feel if he got off on a technicality.' He picked up his coat. 'Okay, now let's go and catch our killer.'

9

A Macabre Discovery

It was ten to four in the morning when the numerous patrol cars and two Black Marias parked up. A score or more policemen, most in riot gear — some armed with submachine guns — got out. Dawn was still an hour or so away and the sky was black. It was cold and there was a chill drizzle in the air. Somewhere far off, a dog was barking.

'Right. We've gone over this a dozen times, so everyone knows what they're doing,' Vaughn said. 'Wilkes, Turner, Theobald and Harley, you're outside at all times, keeping an eye on the back door. Hansby, Rogers and Tyler, you're with me. I want this done professionally, by the book. No slip-ups. The remainder of you stay here as back-up and man the road blocks. The bastard mustn't be allowed to get away. Once we get inside,

I'll take the lead. The suspect's probably armed, so use extra caution.'

Like a sergeant major examining his troops on parade, Vaughn looked at each of his men in turn. He threw away his cigarette. 'It's also possible that his grandmother's inside, though I don't see her causing any problems. Now let's do this.'

The orders given, the eight policemen stealthily filed out. Using low walls as cover and clinging to the shadows, they made their way slowly towards the house. Vaughn and Tyler, both authorised firearm officers, had their guns holstered, ready to use as and when the need arose.

The drizzle was becoming heavier.

The three-storey terraced house was in darkness. The properties on either side, like many on the street, looked abandoned; boarded up and condemned.

Vaughn glanced at his wristwatch. He waited a few minutes.

'They should be in place at the rear of the building by now, sir,' said Tyler.

Radio contact was made a few seconds later, confirming this.

'We're ready to go when you are, sir,'

Tyler declared somewhat nervously.

Vaughn nodded. 'Okay, Hansby. Show-time.'

At six-foot-seven and weighing in at over three hundred and fifty pounds, Constable Colin Hansby was the biggest policeman in the Greater Manchester Constabulary — a veritable powerhouse of a man who primarily served on the football terraces, where he had a reputation of beating sense into many a hooligan. Hefting a huge sledgehammer, he walked calmly up to the front door and with one hefty two-handed swing, smashed it open, knocking it off its hinges.

Vaughn charged forward. 'Police! Police!' he yelled at the top of his voice, storming through the wrecked doorway and into the narrow hallway, the others cramming in behind him.

Tyler threw the light switch but it had no effect.

Torches were pulled out and, in the bright beams of light, doors were forced open. Shadows danced eerily.

Apart from the rats and the cock-roaches that laired here in abundance, the ground floor was deserted. It was filthy and it stank. Mildewed wallpaper sloughed off the walls in great patches like diseased skin from a leper. Many of the windows were broken.

The lounge was especially bad. The sofa was torn and shabby, and what other furniture there was looked decades old and in a similar state of decrepitude. In one corner a heap of rubbish, comprised mainly of filthy articles of clothing, lay piled up almost to the ceiling. On a small table, gathering mould and maggots, were the revolting remains of a months-old half-eaten dinner.

'God!' exclaimed Tyler.

'The kitchen's one hell of a mess, but there's nobody there,' said Hansby.

Behind him, pale-faced and gagging, Constable Paul Rogers looked as though he was about to faint.

'Upstairs!' Vaughn ordered. Leaving the disgusting lounge, he re-entered the hall and made for the narrow staircase. The stairs creaked ominously as he began the ascent and, with each tread, he feared he would collapse through into some terrible dark cellar, whereupon he would be set upon by a horde of ravenous rats. He shone his torch up, half-expecting, half-dreading that he would see the Grim Reaper on the landing, and it would not be gripping a scythe but a double-barrelled shotgun. With one pull of the trigger it would blast him apart, spraying the damp walls with his blood and glistening innards.

'I'm right behind you, sir,' said Tyler.

The landing was notably tidier, leading Vaughn to think that the ground floor was intentionally squalid in order to give the impression, certainly to a casual visitor, that the place was abandoned. Four doors, all closed, lay before them. At the far end the landing turned a corner, beyond which a second flight of stairs led up to the top floor.

The fact that no one had challenged their intrusion suggested two things to Vaughn. Either there was no one here, or — and this was the thought that concerned him — the killer was waiting, perhaps skulking in the shadows or lurking behind a closed door, ready to strike. With a nervous gulp, he signalled for Tyler to halt, then drew his gun. Edging towards the nearest door, he stopped and listened, trying to pick out any sounds that might betray the murderer's whereabouts.

Aside from the low creaks as Hansby and Rogers crept up the stairs, all was quiet.

The blood was pounding in Vaughn's ears as he moved into position and handed Tyler the torch. For the briefest of moments, he was unsure as to whether he should quietly turn the door handle or just boot the door in. Opting for the latter, he gave the frame a powerful kick and immediately assumed a shooting position, gun in both hands. There was a sudden flash of movement that startled him and almost caused him to fire, but it was only his reflection in a grimy bathroom mirror directly opposite.

The bathroom was small and untidy, but not on a par with the uninhabitable conditions downstairs. Still, the owner would be winning no prizes for hygiene. From the basic toiletries and the state of the bath, the sink and the unflushed toilet, it was pretty obvious that the room had been used within the last day or two.

Systematically, the remaining three rooms — two small bedrooms and an even smaller storage space that had been converted into a crude kitchen — were entered. All were empty, though there were enough tell-tale signs to show that they had been recently occupied. In the makeshift kitchen, in which a cooking stove had been set up, there was a bag of freshly bought groceries and several unopened cans of beer.

Vaughn's heart was beating fast as he approached the stairs leading further up. Not one to frighten easily, he still felt as though his legs had become like lead weights. Willing himself onwards, taking some comfort in the company of the men around him and the gun in his hand, he moved to the end of the landing, convinced now that the murderer was close at hand.

The one and only time he had been in a situation like this had ended at about this point in the proceedings when the suspect, realising the game was up, had turned his gun on himself. This time Vaughn knew — he just knew — that things would be different; that suicide was not how Michael Brooks would end this.

Tyler crept to his superior's side in readiness.

'Brooks!' Vaughn called out. 'If you're up there, I want you to come quietly. The place is surrounded by armed police. There's no way out. Hand yourself in and no one will get hurt.'

The warning went unanswered.

'I'm giving you one last chance. It's all over. If you fail to surrender, you will be shot.'

Still no reply.

Vaughn let out his pent-up breath. Steeling himself, he peeked around the corner and risked a glance up the stairs.

It was dark and shadowy.

There was an unpleasant tightening sensation in Vaughn's stomach. From somewhere above came what sounded like a creaking floorboard — a sound which started a small germ of panic screaming deep within his brain.

Then, in direct contrast to the clamorous assault which had accompanied the pre-dawn raid, all was quiet once more.

Enough of this, thought Vaughn. With a nod to his team, he leapt from his position and led the headlong rush up the narrow stairs. At the top there was a short corridor with two closed doors — one to the right, one to the left. Without waiting, he shouldered the one on the left open and stepped back immediately, startled, yet not entirely surprised at the scene before him. As Tyler shone his torch inside, the details became more apparent.

'Christ!' Tyler exclaimed.

Part study, part darkroom, the area into which the two detectives entered contained all the evidence they needed to confirm that this was the correct address, and, more importantly, to put Brooks away for a long time. The walls were covered with numerous photographs and sketched portraits of the deceased: Kemp, Forrester, Willoughby, Father Kelly and Moira Stillwell. Disturbingly, alongside this gallery of the deceased there were dozens of photographs of schoolboys, all but one of which had been defaced with a large red cross.

The unblemished photograph was of Brian Garwood.

On a desk there were several photograph albums, again all featuring images of those that had been murdered. A heavy binder contained many scribbled pages of dates and place names. A large ornate cabinet — the one Vaughn had seen in Kugelbreck's photograph housing the six dolls — lay empty against the wall.

'Next room!' Pushing Tyler aside, Vaughn charged back into the corridor and threw his weight against the unopened door, surprised to find it locked. He stepped back and shouldered it a second time, more firmly, and the door smashed open. What he saw in that first instant, even though it was shrouded in shadow, brought a horrified scream to his lips and caused him to involuntarily fire off three bullets.

★ ★ ★

'I've never seen anything like it. It's . . . it's like something out of a horror film.' Grimacing, Hughes stood, arms crossed, staring at the unsightly thing in the chair. 'I think it's safe to assume this is the preserved corpse of Brooks's grandmother.' Despite his medical training and his long years of handling cadavers, he gulped as he raised a leathery, withered grey arm, noting the thin metal strut that ran alongside it, supporting it. The heavily wrinkled cadaverous face had been powdered with make-up, and there were traces of recently applied lipstick.

Four hours had passed since the macabre discovery, and Vaughn still found it unnerving to look at the remains of Miriam von Beck. This went way beyond madness — part embalmed corpse, part mechanical being; a ghastly moth-eaten, shawl-covered hybrid creation. The product of an insane genius, its head and dead limbs proved capable of a rudimentary animation thanks to an intricate clockwork system. Indeed, it had already been stirred into life when

Vaughn had inadvertently triggered the start-up mechanism. The manner in which it had jerked into motion, the head turning from side to side with both arms rising in a robotic manner, had caused him to back away in fear and was certain to fuel future nightmares. What had been equally disturbing was the spine-tingling harpsichord music — the old-fashioned tinkling jewellery-box tune that had accompanied its bizarre movements.

'Well . . . believe it or not, what we've got here is a dead body that has been partially transformed into an automaton. As I said, I've never seen anything like it.' Hughes remained flabbergasted. He stepped back from it and removed his plastic gloves. 'It's probably the strangest thing I've ever seen. I'm not sure whether she should be buried or exhibited in the Black Museum. The body's been reasonably well embalmed, clearly by someone who knew what they were doing. As for how long she's been like this . . . it's hard to say. Several months . . . maybe a year.'

'Okay,' Vaughn sighed. 'Just when I

thought things couldn't get any stranger, it now seems that Brooks is a cross between Norman Bates and Dr Frankenstein.'

Tyler entered the squalid bedroom. 'We've now got all the evidence out of the other room, sir. However, there's no sign of the sixth doll. What we *have* found is this.' He removed a black-and-white photograph of a tall, slim youth with black hair and piercing eyes — a young Bela Lugosi if there ever was one — who stood alongside an elderly woman in the same patterned shawl the corpse was draped in. Written on the back was: 'Yigael and Miriam von Beck. Manchester. 1958.'

Vaughn took the photograph. 'Excellent! We'll get this circulated as soon as possible. Right. I think the best thing we can do at the moment is start going through this stuff back at the station. We've got some breathing space now that the boy's safe, but we can't afford to sit idle — there's one hell of a crazy individual still at large, so I want this place to be kept under surveillance at all times in the hope that he returns.' He nodded to the nonagenarian mummy. 'If he's a good boy, he'll no doubt want to come and check on his gran.' Leaving the room, he took a deep breath and started down the stairs. He paused at the front door and shook his head, hoping he would never have to set foot again in this house of horrors.

'I don't know about you, but I'm glad to be out of there,' Tyler said. 'It didn't half give me the creeps.'

'Come on, let's get back to the station.' Hands in pockets, Vaughn stalked towards his parked car, his detective sergeant by his side. 'You know, I'm not sure what Wishbourne's going to make of all this. Like me, he no doubt thought we'd have our suspect by now. He's not going to be pleased.'

'It's just occurred to me, sir . . . ' Tyler hesitated.

'What?'

'Well, if this Brooks is as mad as he appears to be, and he needs to get to his last victim, is it possible that if he becomes aware we've got him under protection, he might launch an attack against the station?'

'Let's hope he does.' Vaughn gave a cold smile. Having now reached his car, he opened the driver's door. 'I wouldn't fancy his — '

It was at that instant that Tyler let out a sharp cry.

Vaughn looked up. There, twenty or so yards away, just turning a street corner, a heavy-looking bag slung over his shoulder, was a man who looked very similar to the one in the photograph. Same build. Same dark hair. Same staring eyes.

For a brief moment it was as though time had stopped.

'Get in!' Vaughn shouted, fumbling for his keys. He started the engine, only vaguely aware that Tyler had managed to leap inside, before slamming his foot down on the accelerator and swinging the car out into the road.

The dark-haired stranger turned and fled.

Speeding down the street, Vaughn then flung the car into a sharp right-hand turn. Tyres screamed as the vehicle spun. A rear light was smashed as the car's back end collided with a lamp-post.

Tyler grabbed the car radio and frantically spoke into it: 'Calling all units! Suspect spotted fleeing along Norton Drive. Headed for Daly Street. Urgent back-up required! I repeat, urgent back-up required!'

Knuckles white around the steering wheel, Vaughn glanced to his right and saw the fleeing figure. Now that they were entering a slightly more residential area, he cursed upon seeing the line of parked cars, for he had intended to swing the car over to either hit or cut off the escapee.

'Look out!' Tyler screamed.

Vaughn hit the brakes and fiercely dragged the steering wheel to one side as an elderly man on a bike appeared from between the parked cars. Missing the cyclist by mere inches, he cursed, hit the accelerator and, swerving around an oncoming milk float, resumed the chase. There was a loud crash behind him; in his rear-view mirror he saw that the milk float, in taking its own evasive action, had overturned and now lay on its side in the middle of the road, its none-too-pleased driver shaking his fist and hurling insults.

Fifty yards up ahead, a lollipop woman had stopped the traffic for a gathering of primary-aged schoolchildren.

Michael Brooks — if indeed it was him — was still running, his movement impeded somewhat by the large bag he was carrying.

The sound of approaching police sirens could be heard, heralding that back-up was on its way.

Vaughn brought the car to a stop and hurriedly got out. Even though he smoked and perhaps drank more than was better for him, he was, certainly for a fifty-one-year-old, in quite good condition. Still, the man he was after had to be at least ten years his junior. Dodging nimbly around a woman pushing a pram, he caught sight of the suspect as he sprinted across the road, narrowly avoided an oncoming bus, then vanished down a side street.

Car horns blared as Tyler, younger and more athletic than his superior, weaved through the traffic.

The police sirens were getting louder, much louder.

Vaughn paused for a moment to catch his breath. The pain of a stitch was lancing through his chest. 'What are you waiting for? Get after him!' Gritting his teeth, he tried to blot out the hurt. 'I'll catch you up.'

Without a moment's hesitation, Tyler took off.

Car doors slammed shut and Vaughn was relieved to see Constables Harley and Theobald running over. More reinforcements were getting out of a squad car on the other side of the road.

Briefly, Vaughn found himself reflecting on how, nine times out of ten, it always ended like this. Days and weeks spent arduously and methodically sifting through the evidence, painstakingly piecing the clues together bit by bit — and it still tended to come down to a race, whether by car or on foot. And, what was more, there were no prizes for coming second. With that thought, he took a deep gasping breath and rejoined the chase.

A sudden gunshot rang out, bringing

all of the policemen to an abrupt standstill.

Vaughn drew out his gun and took cover in a butcher's shop doorway. With vigorous hand movements, he gestured to his men to get down. Scanning the side street, he was pleased to see Tyler sheltering behind a parked car a hundred yards or so away.

A second shot went off. Then Tyler was up and running again.

Breathing heavily, the air now rasping from his aching lungs, Vaughn did his best to keep up, but the pace the suspect set was punishing. What he would give right now for an experienced police dog handler to turn up — see how the escapee managed with seventy pounds of German Shepherd dog snapping at his rear.

How the man managed to run as fast as he did carrying that heavy-looking bag was anyone's guess. It was clear that whatever was inside was of importance, otherwise surely it would have been ditched by now.

It seemed to Vaughn that everything

was happening too quickly, bordering on the unreal. At one point he nearly tripped, but managed to save himself from a nasty fall by catching hold of a lamp-post. Houses, cars, trees and screaming people passed by in featureless blurs as he ran on. One minute he was dashing down a cobbled road that reminded him of Coronation Street, a scruffy couple resembling Stan and Hilda Ogden directing him on. The next minute he was tearing across a children's playground, oblivious to the many gawking stares. Then he was sprinting along another road before coming out in a rundown shopping precinct, where the ground was littered with discarded plastic carrier bags, crumpled beer cans and dog excrement.

People were yelling. Dogs were barking. Things were becoming chaotic. Yet still the chase went on. Theobald seemed to be gaining ground.

The strong aroma of Chinese food assaulted Vaughn's nostrils as he passed an alley where an old Asian man was emptying a takeaway's bins.

Two further shots echoed within the built-up area.

Turning a corner, Vaughn saw Tyler leaning against a wall, moments before his detective sergeant slumped to the ground.

'Bastard's shot me,' Tyler shouted unbelievingly, his face pale. Blood trickled from between the fingers clamped to his right shoulder. 'I've been — ' His head sagged to one side and he passed out.

'Harley, stay with Tyler,' Vaughn ordered.

Up ahead, a violent struggle was taking place. Vaughn could see Theobald tussling with the dark-haired man, the large bag having now been finally dashed to the ground. He froze immediately as the suspect grabbed the constable around the neck and pointed his gun to the side of his head.

'Any closer and he gets it!'

'Whoa! Wait a minute.' Vaughn took a few steps closer.

'Drop your gun!'

Theobald squirmed but his captor had a firm hold.

'I said, drop your gun.'

'Just — ' Vaughn started.

'Do it now, I tell you, or I'll kill him!'

Reluctantly, Vaughn dropped his gun. 'Okay. Now let him go.'

'I will . . . in exchange for the boy.'

'So you *are* Michael Brooks.'

'Yes. Now hand over the boy. Give me the boy and I'll let him go.'

'What boy?'

'Don't play the fool with me. The boy you have at the station. I've been out all night trying to figure out how to get him, but now . . . well, you've no choice but to hand him over.'

'You can't have him,' Vaughn said quietly, with a shake of his head.

'But I must! You don't understand. You'll never understand.' There was a desperate glint in Brooks's eyes. 'He's the last of them.'

Vaughn could hear more sirens. 'This place will soon be swarming with policemen. You'll never get away. Let my constable go, throw down your gun and come quietly.'

'I can't!' Brooks screeched. He looked around warily, checking that there was no one sneaking up on him. 'Get me the boy or I'll kill him here and now.'

Theobald had a wife and a young family, and the thought of him being sacrificed in this manner pained Vaughn deeply. As a last resort, he tried shock tactics. 'Yigael von Beck. Your grandmother sends a message for you.'

Brooks' jaw dropped open and just for a second he loosened his grip on Theobald.

The constable wrenched himself away, and the shot that Brooks instinctively fired grazed the side of his neck instead of killing him. The wounded constable crumpled to the ground. Raising his gun, Brooks fired at the detective. Vaughn felt the bullet whiz past his right ear.

Anger consumed him, lending him a sudden burst of strength. Rushing forward, he sprang at Brooks, grabbing him around the waist in a savage rugby tackle, knocking him to the ground. Punches were exchanged, and then Brooks was scrambling to get free. Grabbing the murderer by a leg, Vaughn pulled fiercely. Brooks shook him off and drove in a vicious kick that caught the detective full in the stomach and knocked the wind from him. He did it again, more savagely.

Rolling in agony, Vaughn caught sight of Harley as he now joined the melee. The police constable's helmet was sent flying. Harley went for a choke hold, but Brooks squirmed free, nipped behind the policeman and thumped in two solid kidney punches. The constable stumbled back a step before jumping in and head-butting his attacker full in the face. Blood squirted as Brooks's nose burst.

Vaughn was now back on his feet. Grabbing the murderer by the hair, he then swung his assailant hard against a betting shop's window. The huge pane of glass shattered on impact. Brooks lay half-inside, half-outside. He moaned for a moment, then lay still.

10

Interview with a Madman

A doctor had checked Brooks over and proclaimed that, physically at least, he was able to be questioned. When Vaughn had flung him through the window, it had knocked him out briefly; but surprisingly, he only had minor cuts from the broken glass. He had come round to find himself in handcuffs in a police car, sandwiched between two constables.

Vaughn had set up the interview room with a tape recorder, a large pot of coffee for himself and Tyler, and three chairs. The detective sergeant had been quickly revived and his shoulder patched up. The doctor had wanted him to go to hospital, but Tyler desperately wanted to sit in on the interview. Vaughn had agreed, with the proviso that he let someone drive him to hospital as soon as they had finished.

Brooks had been charged with five

counts of murder for the time being. They had puzzled over whether possession of the automated remains of Miriam von Beck constituted a crime, but decided to shelve that decision until later on. Two burly constables were stationed just inside the door, ready to intervene if Brooks became violent again. From the look in their eyes, Vaughn knew they were hoping he would.

In a box on the floor was the doll that had been recovered from the scene of Keith Kemp's death. The remaining four dolls and the child doll, which they had found in Brooks's bag, were being kept in the evidence room. The bag had also contained a black cloak, leather gloves and a white full-face mask with features painted on it in a similar manner to those of the dolls.

Vaughan took a last look round the room and nodded in satisfaction. He turned to the constables. 'Okay, tell Hansby to bring the suspect in.' He sat down next to Tyler and waited.

Brooks walked in with a worried expression on his face. He looked ill and nervy, his skin more grey than olive now that he had been captured. Hansby seated him opposite Vaughn and then left the room.

Vaughn turned on the tape recorder and cleared his throat before stating the date and time. It was now well after eleven o'clock, but the morning sunlight would not penetrate the small windowless room. He felt energised by all that had happened, though he knew it would soon fade, and he wanted to start questioning Brooks while the man was still tired and in pain from his injuries.

'Can you confirm that you are Michael Brooks of nineteen Ackerman's Lane?' he began.

'Yes,' Brooks answered.

'I will ask you again if you would like to have a legal representative present.'

'No. There's no point.'

'Okay. Mr Brooks, you've been charged with five counts of murder, one count of conspiracy to murder, and several charges relating to the events surrounding your arrest. We've found evidence at your address that clearly links you to the murders, and the eye witness evidence of at least five policemen who saw, and in some cases experienced, your violent attempts to resist arrest. Do you have anything to say to the charges?'

Brooks slid down a little in his chair as if very tired. Tipping his head back, he took a deep breath. 'It's true,' he said. 'All of it's true.'

Vaughn was only slightly surprised by the admission of guilt. Brooks would never be able to wriggle out of the charges. The evidence against him was just too strong. He glanced at Tyler to see how he was coping with the shoulder injury and got a look of grim satisfaction in return.

'We know a lot about you, Michael, and about your family. We know that your birth name was Yigael von Beck and that at some point that was changed to Michael Brooks. We know you lived with your grandmother and that you did national service, training as a sapper, when you were eighteen. What we don't know is exactly why you chose to take the lives of five innocent people. Your co-operation now might serve to lessen your sentence, so I strongly suggest you tell us everything.'

Vaughn was keeping his tone of voice level, but it was difficult. Images of the victims kept invading his mind. What he really wanted was to get an explanation of the crimes for the families. In his opinion, Brooks was heading for a lifetime spent in a psychiatric unit, regardless of the information he gave them.

'Where to begin?' Brooks said wearily. 'There's so much I have to tell you.'

'Why don't you start with Keith Kemp? Your first victim,' Vaughn said.

'No. You're thinking about this the wrong way.' Brooks shook his head irritably. 'First of all, I was never Yigael von Beck. Not officially. My parents had already adopted the name Brooks before I was born. It's only my grandmother who calls me that. She says we need to remember who we really are. She brought me up, you know; taught me all about my heritage, my religion. Our family was important once. My grandfather, Salomon, was a respected man with a big house and servants. It broke her heart when he never made it to England.'

'This was when the family fled Vienna,' Vaughn said, noting that Brooks spoke of Miriam as if she was still alive.

'Yes. He sent them ahead — Miriam, Jacob and Ruth — to a friend in London. He was trying to find a buyer for his house to get some money to set us up properly. From the rumours we heard, he was sold out to the Nazis by a rival, and they sent him to Mauthausen-Gusen concentration camp to die. The only thing that followed us to England was those damned dolls.' Brooks's face had lost some of its tiredness as it took on a look of hatred.

'How exactly did that happen?' Vaughn asked.

'Salomon had packed up some of the treasures, the larger stuff that couldn't be easily carried. He arranged for them to be shipped to London, but all the crates were confiscated — all except for the dolls. They took months to get to us but they found us in the end. Apparently my father was pleased to see them. He knew they had been made by his grandfather and were valuable. He planned to sell them and move us out of London, but every time he thought he had a buyer, something went wrong. It's like they didn't want to be sold. He was supporting the family by doing jewellery repairs, but he needed cash to be able to make his own pieces. Then I was born, in March of 1941. My parents named me Michael and my grandmother named me Yigael.'

'Interesting though this is, can we fast forward a bit? If we're going to have a year-by-year account, we'll be here a very long time,' said Vaughn. The psychologists could sort all of this stuff out. He wanted to get to more recent events.

'But you need to know why I had to kill the dolls!' Brooks protested.

'No, I need to know why you killed the people,' Vaughn corrected acerbically.

'You don't get it!' Brooks was exasperated. 'Those things were not people!'

Tyler couldn't contain his anger at that. The pain from his shoulder was insistent, despite the medication he had been given. 'Of course they were, and you know it. I

220

think you're trying to plead insanity when you're actually just a murdering bastard who gets off on slaughter.'

'That's a lie!' Brooks insisted. 'Let me tell you. Once you know the whole story, you'll understand,' he pleaded.

'All right. Keep going then,' Vaughn said, locking gazes with Brooks. 'But speed it up a bit.'

Brooks took a deep breath and angled himself so he was able to avoid Tyler's glare somewhat. 'In April 1941, the rooms where we lived were bombed. My grandmother and I were at a friend's house and we got stuck there when the sirens started. We survived, but my parents didn't. Hardly anything of ours was retrievable. Yet, amidst the ruin, undamaged, was the cabinet containing the dolls. Nothing else. Just it, lying there in the bomb crater.'

'That cabinet must have been well made,' Vaughn commented neutrally, mostly to see what effect it would have on Brooks.

'It's antique hardwood, but that's not the point. The dolls *couldn't* have been killed, not like that. We've tried! You see it was then, when the firemen pulled the cabinet out of the rubble, that my grandmother first began to have her suspicions.' Brooks had completely lost his look of fatigue and instead seemed animated by whatever obsession it was that had brought him to that point. 'Only two people died in that bombing raid — my parents. All the others on our street were just injured, but our home was flattened. My grandmother was devastated. All her family were dead except for me. She was in a country she didn't understand, and there were too many who didn't take kindly to Jews.'

'Why didn't she throw the dolls away if she hated them?' Vaughn asked.

'Because she couldn't. At first she sold them to a pawnbroker, but he returned them two days later and demanded his money back. He said they had been putting customers off. She tried giving them away, but no one who got one kept it for long. Even people with no connection to the dolls come to notice that they're evil. You must have felt it yourself.' Brooks appealed to Vaughn, his eyes intense.

Vaughn was not going to admit to finding them creepy, but even his slight pause was seized on by Brooks.

'I can see it in your eyes! You *do* know what I mean.'

'Oh, come off it! They're just dolls. A bit of porcelain and some cloth, that's all,' Tyler scoffed.

'Then why have they tried to kill us so many times?' Brooks shot back at Tyler. 'Ever since I was a boy they've haunted us. We moved up to Birmingham first and we left them behind, but someone sent them on to us. Just after they arrived, my grandmother fell down the stairs and broke her hip. I had meningitis as a child. I got knocked down by a car. Our flat in Birmingham caught fire. They were trying to kill us!'

'But why do you think that?'

'Because all the von Becks should have died in Vienna.' Brooks clung onto the table, his fingertips white. 'We shouldn't have tried to escape our fate. The dolls tried to finish us off, and they took my parents and my grandfather, but they won't get me. We finally found a way to kill them. She worked it out.'

'She? Do you mean Miriam?' Vaughn asked. He had heard some strange confessions in his time, but this one took the biscuit, and more than once he had looked at the recorder to check it was working. If Brooks chose to clam up later on and they had not got it on tape, a jury would never believe it.

'Yes. She's never stopped trying to save me. After I'd finished in the army, we moved to Manchester, and it was then that she knew. I came home one day and she told me she'd seen one of the dolls in its other form, its vulnerable form. She had seen the 'Tavern Owner' doll in the newspaper.'

'That would be Malcolm Forrester?'

'Yes. It was undeniably him. You see, we knew there had to be a way the dolls were causing the accidents, and finally we saw how. They had counterparts who looked human, but weren't. Evil-spirited twins. Doppelgängers.'

From where he sat, Vaughn could see

the two constables on guard. They were watching the suspect for any signs that he could turn violent, and their faces were mostly impassive, but he saw them exchange a look that clearly indicated they thought Brooks was completely cracked. Vaughn agreed. He had met a few genuinely insane men in the course of his career, and one or two fakers. This was the real deal all right.

The grandmother had lost it when her family was destroyed and had inculcated Brooks with her own paranoid obsession. Vaughn's job now was to complete the interview and fill in the blanks in the investigation. Then he could hand Brooks over to the shrinks.

'So you found Forrester first. What about the others?' he asked, jotting down a few notes.

'It took me a long time — years in fact, but as all the counterparts had to live close to us to keep in contact with the dolls, I knew I would eventually spot them. The boy was the hardest. I only found that one last month. I had to have everything in place before I started the campaign. If there's one thing I learned in the army, it was preparation. The dolls would be aware that I was posing a threat to them and they would take steps. I never would have managed it without my grandmother.' Brooks paused, looked at his watch once again and pointed at the coffee pot. 'Do you think I could have a drink?' he asked. 'I'm quite thirsty.'

Vaughn shrugged, poured a cup of coffee and waited while Brooks took a sip. 'Carry on. What help did she give you?'

'In order to destroy the dolls, I had to first get rid of their killable counterparts.' Brooks put his cup down. 'Are you with me so far?'

'Like voodoo, but the other way round?' Tyler said, his curiosity briefly overcoming his contempt for the suspect.

'Exactly! Well, as soon as the first one had been completed, the dolls would've known. We had to trick them. She prayed constantly for guidance, and even when she was getting ill she wouldn't stray from our task. She's a very knowledgeable woman. I mean, I don't suppose you've ever heard of the golems — the animated beings from Jewish folklore?'

Vaughn shook his head. 'Strangely enough, no. Can't say that I want to either.'

'Well she knew all about them, and realised that the doppelgängers were similar. If she were to die of natural causes, as seemed increasingly likely, the dolls would switch all their attention to me. If, however, we could find a way to change her into a being that is neither dead nor alive, they would be confused.'

'I'm sorry, but I'm the one who's confused. What exactly did you do to your grandmother?' Vaughn asked, half-dreading the answer.

'Oh, don't worry. She's all right, Inspector. She's just in a trance-like state,' Brooks said with complete sincerity. 'Once I've killed all the dolls I'll revive her.'

'You'll . . . revive her?' Vaughn repeated, his voice deadpan.

'Yes, she's fine; she's told me so. We went over the idea many times, and one day I came home to find that she'd achieved the trance. I knew then that it was time to put our plans in motion.'

'And so you killed Keith Kemp on his way to work.'

'I followed all the doppelgängers and knew just when to strike. It all went well.'

'And then Malcolm Forrester? How did you get into the factory?'

'He let me in. I said I had a message from his son, so he opened the door and walked ahead of me. I had the chance to hit him on the head, so I took it. There was no one around.'

Tyler joined in again. 'Did you *intend* to spear Simon Willoughby with the scaffolding?'

'Yes, of course I did. That's what my grandmother told me to do. She was very specific. Although I admit I was surprised when it went right through him. The only time he was vulnerable was walking to and from work, so I had to strike then.' Brooks glanced at his watch again.

'Sorry, are we keeping you from something? An appointment with your bank manager, perhaps?' Vaughn asked sarcastically.

'It's just a habit.'

'Then get on with it.'

'Very well. The priest was easier. He drank too much and never noticed when I followed him. I had to wait until he was fully dressed up, though, and that meant I had to get him in his church. That one was messy . . . the doll kept squirming.'

'And finally, Moira Stillwell,' Vaughn prompted, sickened, but determined to see it through to the end before halting the interview.

'Is that her name? It didn't matter. She was the one.' Brooks was unemotional about the killings, detached from their violence.

'Did you always intend to lock her in the freezer? To let her die a horrifyingly slow death?' Vaughn tried to prod Brooks into engaging with his actions.

'I wouldn't have done that if there hadn't been a struggle.' Brooks looked affronted. 'I broke into the kitchen when the others had left. I thought I could knock her out first. The doll was screaming, so I had to shut them both up.'

He had been getting jumpy — checking his watch, twisting the material of his shirt and glancing nervously at the door. Suddenly he leaped to his feet and the two constables started forward, ready to grab him.

'What does it matter now?' Brooks cried. 'I've failed. It only needs one doll left alive to kill me. You've condemned me to death! Do you realise that? You've got the final counterpart here, under your bloody protection. Well, who is going to protect *me*?'

'Just what do you think is going to happen to you? How can a doll possibly hurt you?' Vaughn asked in disbelief.

'If I can't kill the doll, it'll kill me!' Brooks shouted. 'I don't know how. It could be a bloody earthquake for all I know.' He sagged back into his chair, seemingly in despair.

Vaughn took a deep breath. Brooks truly believed the insane rubbish he was spewing out. There was little more to learn from the man, for his purposes at least. The families of the victims would have some measure of relief from knowing he was never going to enjoy freedom again. He would be kept indefinitely at Broadmoor or one of the other high-security mental hospitals. Or if by some miracle he was judged to be of sound mind, he would be serving more years than he had left to him.

'I'm going to pause this interview for the moment.' Vaughn reached for the recorder to turn it off.

'Wait! I want to know what you're going to do with me!' Brooks protested, his eyes wild.

'We'll return you to your cell,' Vaughn replied dispassionately, and switched off the machine.

'No! He'll get to me there! At least if I'm with other people I've some protection.' Brooks was shaking with genuine fear.

'I've had enough of this, Brooks.'

'But I can tell you more!'

'You will, but not right now.' Vaughn was disgusted with the murderer. There may have been good reason for his insanity, but plenty of people coped with worse trauma without killing people.

'I must tell you everything!' Brooks wailed.

Vaughn had heard quite enough. This interview was in direct contrast with most that he had conducted. The suspects usually insisted on waiting for their lawyers, and even then all you could get out of them was 'no comment' repeated ad nauseam.

The problem with Brooks was not persuading him to talk, it was persuading him to shut up. Vaughn suspected he was now just prevaricating to forestall returning to his cell.

* * *

Hughes would be the first to admit he felt uncomfortable with the knowledge that the semi-mechanical corpse of Miriam von Beck was, at the moment, propped undignifiedly against the wall, the black body bag in which she had been wrapped for transportation now lying open at her shrivelled feet. In his professional capacity he had seen countless cadavers, though there was a look to this dead woman's face that was unnerving. It was almost as though she knew something he did not.

Shaking his head, trying to rid himself of his unwelcome thoughts, he headed over to the large counter, atop which were the items that had been recovered from Brooks's holdall. The sixth doll, the doll of the boy, had felt different, heavier, and it warranted further investigation. He reached for a magnifying glass.

There came a knock at the door. Hughes turned. 'Come — '

With a final, barely audible click, the countdown expired and the long-delay timer triggered the detonation of the five pounds of gelignite that had been expertly packed inside the last doll. There was a deafening roar as the small evidence room, Hughes and the unfortunate policeman who had just entered were blown to pieces, consumed in the expanding fireball. The walls were blasted apart and the door was thrown twenty yards down the corridor. In the blink of an eye, the accumulated evidence from countless crimes was obliterated.

The entire left wing of the station

rocked as though struck by a high magnitude earthquake. Everywhere, windows shattered. Fire alarms rang out. People were coughing and screaming, trying to flee the fire and the billowing black smoke. Others stood — bloody, confused, shell-shocked; unable to comprehend what had happened.

The interrogation room was but two doors down from the epicentre of the explosion, and Vaughn and Tyler were both sent flying from their seats. The overhead light fell from its mooring and shattered on the central table. There were papers everywhere, scattered on the floor and spiralling in the air. A portion of the ceiling caved in. Of the two policemen by the door, both were struck unconscious, having been hurled into the wall by the shockwave.

With a loud crash, much of the floor directly above where the bomb had gone off — the administrative department — collapsed, killing three secretaries and burying many others.

The injured crawled and clawed their way through the devastation.

'Jesus Christ!' cursed Vaughn, unsteadily getting to his feet, the noise of the blast still ringing in his ears. He was covered in dust. Blood trickled down the side of his face from where something must have hit him. Rubbing his eyes, he stared about him. For a moment his vision swam, and it was hard to focus. He saw an approaching blur — and then Brooks was pushing him aside, rushing out into the corridor. For a split second, Vaughn was too stunned to notice.

Smoke billowed out of the station: a huge, acrid, dense black cloud.

Those fortunate not to be numbered among the casualities made for the emergency exits. Others clambered out of windows. The well-rehearsed evacuation procedure lay in tatters as the desperate sought any means of escape. The fire alarms continued to blare.

Vaughn heard coughing and turned, relieved to see that Tyler was alive. 'That bastard! He's done this. That's what he was waiting for. I'm going to kill him!' He stumbled out of the room.

The sight that met him was sickening.

Friends and colleagues were lying dead or injured. Much of the building in which he had spent most of his adult life was now reduced to fiery rubble. Though it was the overwhelming sense of shock that really got to him — the stupefied, horror-stricken, blank stares of usually highly disciplined individuals. In one moment of madness everything had drastically changed.

Emerging from the smoke was the tall figure of Constable Hansby, Lockwood slung over one shoulder in a fireman's lift. 'What the hell's happened?' he asked.

'It was a bomb. It must have been in the doll,' Vaughn answered urgently. 'Brooks has escaped, though he can't have got far. Once you've seen to Lockwood, round up as many men as you can and start searching. He mustn't be allowed to get away.' Without waiting for a reply, Vaughn turned and ran in the direction he had seen the murderer take. It was then that he was struck with a terrible realisation.

Odds were Brooks had no intention of escaping — not when his final victim remained close at hand, if indeed he and his parents had not been killed in the explosion. Despite Brooks's apparent eagerness to avoid arrest, perhaps that had been his intention all along. After all, what better way of getting within striking distance of his victim? With that disturbing thought, Vaughn sped up, making for the small room off the canteen in which Brian Garwood and his family had been temporarily housed. From outside came the sound of approaching fire engines.

Brooks was a fanatic — a man prepared to go to any lengths to follow his warped beliefs, and Vaughn knew there was only one way of stopping him. Quickly entering his office, he dashed to his desk, and got his gun and a round of bullets. His hands were shaking as he hastily loaded the gun. Then he was out in the main corridor once more, making his way towards the canteen at the far end. The fire alarms came to an abrupt stop.

The canteen door was wide open. The prone body of the policeman who had been assigned guard duty lay nearby. Vaughn rushed forward.

The boy's father lay slumped in a corner, blood streaming from his face, his spectacles cracked and askew on his brow. Mrs Garwood was unconscious, sprawled on the tiled floor.

Brooks stood in the centre of the room, violently shaking the teenager, screaming into his face: 'Why aren't you dead? The doll's dead, why aren't you?'

'Let the boy go!' Vaughn shouted. He raised his gun.

Oblivious to the order, Brooks continued to question the terrified boy. 'Why are you still alive?' Utterly confused, he stumbled back a couple of steps, taking his captive with him. Any reason he had left was slipping away from him. He looked blank; dead, almost. Like one of his dolls. 'I don't understand . . . is there no way out?'

Realising that a delicate procedure was in operation, a crowd of policemen, including Tyler, silently gathered in the doorway to the canteen.

'Let the boy go!' Vaughn repeated.

Brooks turned. 'But he's not dead. Why's he not dead?'

'Let him go!' Vaughn's grip on his gun tightened. His eyes narrowed, and deep down there was a strong part of him that yearned to take the shot, to just squeeze the trigger and bring this nightmarish case to an end. After all, even with the boy employed as a human shield, Brooks still presented a very hittable target, and Vaughn was a good shot. Still, the risk was too great.

Groggily, Brooks shook his head. Things had not gone as planned. Had his grandmother misled him? 'I'll . . . I'll break his neck. He has to die,' he mumbled, although there was little conviction in his voice.

'If you're going to kill the boy, then go ahead and do it.' Vaughn knew he was taking perhaps the biggest gamble of his life, but it was one that he was prepared to take. 'But before you do, think about this — the last of the dolls is dead, killed prior to the death of its double. You've messed up, Michael. Killing the boy won't save you. You know that as well as I do.'

'But I . . . '

'You've failed. Admit it.'

For all his cold, methodical planning, Brooks began to see that he *had* made a grave, fundamental mistake. Both the doll and the boy should have been 'killed' at the same time and in a similar manner. The boy should have died as had the doll. The doll had been blown to pieces. Breaking his hostage's neck would not negate the curse he had lived under all of his life.

'Come on, Michael. Do the right thing and let him go.'

'You don't understand,' Brooks whimpered. 'It's . . . it's either him or me.' His deranged mind was desperately thinking things through, trying to work out if there was some way of salvaging the situation. His eyes were scanning the room, seeing if there was anything nearby that could cause an impromptu explosion. His eyes fell briefly on the small oven in the corner, but he had to be realistic — there was no practical way that would suffice, certainly not whilst he remained at gunpoint.

At that moment, Mr Garwood got to

THE DOPPELGÄNGER DEATHS

While investigating a fatal car crash, Detective Inspector Vaughn's interest is piqued when forensic evidence points to murder, and he is shown the eerie antique doll found sitting on the passenger seat. The blood-spattered doll bears an extraordinary resemblance to the dead man, and on its lap is an envelope containing the message: 'One down. Five to go.' When a second doll is discovered beside another murder victim, the desperate race is then on to find and stop the killer from completing the set of six murders . . .